What the critics are saying...

"Ms. LaFleur creates characters who scintillate and burn so hotly for each other that it is difficult to draw a breath while reading about them." ~ *Coffee Time Romance*

"An absolutely delightful story. I highly recommend RENT-A-STUD." ~ *Romance Reviews Today*

"Be prepared to let RENT-A-STUD escort you through a night of passion with 100% satisfaction guaranteed!" ~ *Euro Reviews*

"RENT-A-STUD, aside from being a sweet love story that would appease even the most die-hard romantic, packs enough steam to make your computer sweat!" ~ *Novelspot*

"Packing just the right touch of emotion to make it touching yet not sappy, and topping if off with a wonderful happily-ever-after ending, Lynn LaFleur's RENT-A-STUD is a little treasure that you will not want to miss." ~ *Just Erotic Romance Reviews*

"RENT-A-STUD is a steamy romp from one page to another." ~ *Joyfully Reviewed*

"This is one of the best older woman-younger man stories I have read. Definitely a book to add to your list next time visiting Ellora's." ~ *Enchanted in Romance*

Lynn LaFleur

RENT-A-STUD

An Ellora's Cave Romantica Publication

www.ellorascave.com

Rent-A-Stud

ISBN # 1419954024

Edited by Raelene Gorlinsky
Cover art by Syneca

Electronic book Publication August 2005
Trade Paperback Publication February 2006

Warning:

The following material contains graphic sexual content meant for mature readers. *Rent-A-Stud* has been rated E–rotic by a minimum of three independent reviewers.

Ellora's Cave Publishing offers three levels of Romantica™ reading entertainment: S (S-ensuous), E (E-rotic), and X (X-treme).

S-*ensuous* love scenes are explicit and leave nothing to the imagination.

E-*rotic* love scenes are explicit, leave nothing to the imagination, and are high in volume per the overall word count. In addition, some E-rated titles might contain fantasy material that some readers find objectionable, such as bondage, submission, same sex encounters, forced seductions, and so forth. E-rated titles are the most graphic titles we carry; it is common, for instance, for an author to use words such as "fucking", "cock", "pussy", and such within their work of literature.

X-*treme* titles differ from E-rated titles only in plot premise and storyline execution. Unlike E-rated titles, stories designated with the letter X tend to contain controversial subject matter not for the faint of heart.

Rent-A-Stud

ꙮ

Trademarks Acknowledgement

~

The author acknowledges the trademarked status and trademark owners of the following wordmarks mentioned in this work of fiction:

Dr Pepper: Dr Pepper/Seven Up, Inc.

Foley's: May Department Stores Company

Lexus: Toyota Jidosha Kabushiki Kaisha Ta Toyota Motor Corporation

Chapter One

ഗ

Zachary Cooper whistled the chorus from "I Can't Get No Satisfaction" as he strolled into the office of Coopers' Companions. The sun shone brightly on this beautiful spring morning. He had his youth, his health, plenty of money in the bank, and he loved his job.

Life simply didn't get any better.

"Mornin', bro," he said.

"Hey, Zach." Brent glanced at his watch. "You're here early."

"Lots to do today. Plus Michelle has something she needs me to sign. I wanted to get that done before I head out to pick up more supplies."

"Still buying materials for your house?"

"Yeah," Zach said with a grin, "and loving every minute of it."

"I'll let you be Stanley Homeowner. I like my apartment. If the plumbing needs fixed, I just call the landlord."

"You have no sense of adventure, little brother."

The telephone's ring put an end to their conversation. Brent picked up the receiver. "Coopers' Companions, this is Brent… Yes, Ms. Talmage, how may I help you?… We have several escorts available Saturday evening. I'm sure you and I can find one to please you." He opened a file folder on his immaculate desk and withdrew a sheet of paper. "I have a few questions to ask you, Ms. Talmage. We want to find the perfect escort for your mother."

Leaving Brent to complete his conversation, Zach wandered across the room and gazed out the window. The house that he and his brother had remodeled for their business was located in an affluent area of Fort Worth, complete with oak, willow, and pecan trees. The trees shaded the house as well as made it eye-pleasing.

The large tree directly outside the office was starting to bloom with fluffy white blossoms. Zach didn't know the name of the tree, but his sister would. Michelle knew the name of every tree, every flower, she'd ever seen. He would swear she could make silk flowers grow. She kept the outside of Coopers' Companions landscaped with a wide assortment of flowers, shrubs, and trees.

She kept the inside of Coopers' Companions as neat and organized as the outside. He and Brent had gladly handed over all the bookwork to Michelle. As COO of the company, she kept the business humming along efficiently and productively.

Plus, they made a shitload of money.

"That sounds great, Ms. Talmage," Zach heard Brent say. "You can be assured your mother will be very pleased with her escort… Thank *you* for calling."

Zach turned to face his brother when he heard Brent end the conversation. "New client?"

"Yeah. One for you."

Sitting on the wide windowsill, Zach crossed his arms over his chest. "Oh?"

"Breanna Talmage asked specifically for you. She said a friend of hers hired you a couple of months ago and was very impressed with your…attention. I take that to mean you fucked her brains out."

He frowned at Brent's choice of words. Sometimes his younger brother's lack of respect for women grated on Zach.

"Not every date ends with sex. You know that from personal experience. Sometimes a woman simply needs an escort, not a stud."

"I know from personal experience that most of them *do* end with sex because that's what the woman wants. No matter the reason for hiring an escort, these women fantasize about a young man fawning over them." He tapped the piece of paper on his desk with one long forefinger. "This one is right up your alley, big brother."

"Who is it?"

Brent turned the paper so he could read it easier. "Her name is Jade Talmage."

Jade. Zach liked that name. It made him think of a sparkling jewel.

"Her daughter is hiring you to escort her mother to some fancy-shmancy shindig at North Texas Highland Hospital." Looking up at his brother, Brent waggled his eyebrows. "Breanna says her mom is a fox."

"All daughters think their mothers are foxes."

"Maybe, but she convinced me her mother really is hot stuff. Thirty-nine years old, chin-length auburn hair, full lips, big green eyes, great legs, voluptuous body." He shivered playfully. "Damn, I'm getting a hard-on." Brent leaned back in his plush leather chair and hooked his hands behind his head. "But since you like the older broads, and since the daughter asked for you, this one is yours."

Zach frowned again. Brent had always thought the best place for a woman was on her back with her legs spread. Zach knew a woman was so much more than just a piece of ass. Rising from the windowsill, he walked to one of the large leather chairs before Brent's desk and sat down. "An older woman is not a 'broad', Brent. All women are beautiful in their own way. They deserve respect and consideration."

"Which is what you give them, and that's why Coopers' Companions is so successful. You're a natural at this, Zach. Tall, good-looking, charming, great sense of humor. The ladies start to salivate as soon as they see you." He grinned. "The fact that you have a big dick doesn't hurt either." Brent leaned forward and picked up the form. "Breanna said her parents divorced almost two years ago. Jade's gone out a few times, but hasn't been involved with anyone since she and her husband split. She should be really horny by the night of your date."

Zach studied his brother. Although only eighteen months younger, Brent had a long way to go before he grew up. Zach knew several twenty-eight-year-old guys who were much more mature than his younger brother. "Do you ever see the *inside* of a woman, Brent?"

"As long as she's gorgeous and a good lay, I don't give a shit what she's like inside. Neither do you. You like sex as much as I do. That's why we started this business."

"I never said I don't like sex. I *love* sex. But I also happen to know there's more to a woman than tits and a pussy." He held out his hand. "When?"

"Saturday night," Brent said, placing the form in Zach's palm. "The daughter's home and cell numbers are on there, too, if you have any questions."

A quick glance at the piece of paper showed him where Breanna's mother lived. He knew the classy, quiet neighborhood in Fort Worth well. "No problem. Jade Talmage and I will get along just fine."

* * * * *

Jade frowned as her daughter held up a silky green thong. "You aren't serious about me wearing that thing."

Breanna's eyes twinkled with a devilish light. "C'mon, Mom, be adventurous. You can't have panty lines in that gorgeous emerald gown."

Jade had bought the emerald gown two weeks ago on her and Breanna's last shopping trip. Now she had second thoughts about it. She wasn't sure if the hospital's Board of Directors would approve of her wearing a dress so revealing. "I'm not sure about that gown, Bre. It's so…low."

"You have incredible cleavage. Show it off."

"I'll be forty in two weeks. I'm a little old to be showing off my cleavage."

"You're a long way from old, Mom. Besides, a beautiful woman is never too old to show off *anything,* and you're a babe."

Jade laughed while her daughter grinned. "A *babe*?"

"Babe, fox, hot stuff. However you say it, you're it."

Jade wrapped her arm around Breanna's shoulders and gave her a quick hug. "I must be doing something right if my twenty-one-year-old daughter thinks I'm hot stuff, even when I need to lose thirty pounds."

"Where?" Breanna's gaze slid over Jade from head to toe and back. "You're perfect, Mom. I wish I had some of your curves." She looked down at her small breasts. "I got your eyes, your nose, your mouth, and Dad's boobs."

Jade's heart swelled with pride when she looked at her stunning daughter. Tall and slim with dark brown hair and olive skin like her father, she turned men's heads wherever she went. "Bre, as slender as you are, you wouldn't be able to stand up straight if you had my breasts."

"That's probably true, but I'd like the chance to find out." Breanna waggled the thong by the elastic straps. The shiny fabric shimmered in the lights. "Speaking of chances, at least try this on, and the matching bra. They're almost the same color as your gown."

Jade wrinkled her nose as she studied the tiny thong. "Those things have to be uncomfortable. Don't they ride up your… You know."

"The word is ass, Mom. It's okay if you say it."

"Hey, I'm old-fashioned. Get used to it."

Breanna chuckled. "I wouldn't have you any other way. But for your information, thongs aren't uncomfortable. I love 'em." She bobbled her eyebrows. "And your date will love it too."

Jade bristled at her daughter's implication. "Breanna Renee, you get that notion out of your head. I let you talk me into having a strange man escort me to the gala tomorrow night—and I still haven't figured out *why* I let you talk me into it—but that's all it is. It isn't a date. Besides, I don't think what he does is even legal."

"There's nothing illegal about being an escort."

"And you think all he does is *escort* women? There's no sex involved?"

"I didn't say that. There's probably sex involved with some women."

"Well, not with this woman. I have no intention of having sex with a man who's paid to pleasure women."

"Maybe you should."

Jade's mouth dropped open. She couldn't believe what her daughter had just said. "*What*?" she squeaked.

"Dad left you two years ago. You get asked out all the time, but I'll bet you haven't had half a dozen dates in that time."

"For your information, I've had several dates in the last two years."

"I doubt if any of those included sex." She tilted her head. "Did they?"

"Breanna!"

"Well, have you had sex or not?"

"No, I haven't," Jade huffed. "There, are you satisfied?" Groaning, she covered her eyes with one hand. "I can't believe I'm having this conversation with my daughter."

Breanna pulled Jade's hand away from her face. "Mom, I'm not a virgin. You know that because I told you about my first time."

"Yes, and I wasn't exactly thrilled with that confession."

Breanna shrugged. "I can't apologize for liking sex. I like it a lot. I inherited that desire from *someone*."

Her ex-husband was a louse for leaving her for a woman fifteen years his junior, but he'd been a wonderful lover. Sex had always been pleasurable for Jade, and she missed it greatly. That didn't mean she'd fall into bed with a man who'd had sex with dozens of other women.

"Two years of celibacy is long enough. Go for it. Do something totally out of character and jump his bones. With all his experience, he's probably incredible in bed."

"He's probably mechanical in bed, making the same moves he believes women love but really loathe." Jade shook her head firmly. "No. He'll be my escort, nothing else. And that's the end of this discussion." She pulled her purse strap higher on her shoulder. "I need shoes and Foley's is having a sale. Let's go."

"What about the underwear?"

"I'll…think about it."

"Which means you'll chicken out."

Jade frowned. "You know, you're not too old to spank for being rude to your mother."

"I'm not being rude, Mom, I just want you to have a good time." She took one of Jade's hands and squeezed it. "I want you to be happy."

The love and concern in Breanna's eyes brought a lump to Jade's throat. Her ex-husband had been a louse, but he'd given her a wonderful daughter. Jade returned Breanna's squeeze. "I appreciate that, and if I meet the right man, I won't have any trouble jumping his bones, okay? But this rent-a-stud isn't the right man."

Chapter Two

"Where are you, Mom?"

"I'm in the bedroom," Jade called out to Breanna.

Jade looked up from the pile of towels she was folding to watch her daughter walk into the room. She couldn't help but notice the large sack her daughter carried from Breanna's favorite bookstore.

"Didn't you buy two books yesterday when we went shopping?"

"*I* don't have a date tonight, so I need *something* to do."

"I told you it isn't a *date,* it's part of my job."

"Pfftt. Details. You're still going out with a hunky man."

"You don't know for sure he's hunky."

"Trust me, Mom. If he works for Coopers' Companions, he's hunky."

"And how do you know that for sure?"

"I told you about Roxanne's date with one of the escorts. She said he was charming and gracious to her, and totally hot."

"I like the charming and gracious part. The totally hot part makes me nervous."

"Why? Are you afraid you won't be able to resist him?"

Jade wiggled her mouth back and forth. "Hardly."

"Don't be logical, Mom. If he's a stud—and I have no doubt he will be—then go for it. Jump his bones and have a good time."

"I thought we finished this conversation yesterday."

"Is that a polite way to tell me to change the subject?"

"I knew I'd raised a smart girl."

"I never get to have any fun." She sat near the end of the bed and opened her bag. "While you're with the hunk, I'll read these erotic romances."

Pushing aside the unfolded towels, Jade crawled up to the middle of the bed and sat facing her daughter. "Some I don't have?"

"Three brand-new ones. I'll let you borrow them after I'm through. You can buy the next ones." A wicked sparkle lit up her eyes. "I did get something for you, though."

Jade wasn't sure if she liked that look in her daughter's eyes. "Should I be afraid?"

"Nah. It's good, I promise."

Reaching into the open bag, Breanna pulled out a smaller, dark maroon sack. Jade recognized the logo on the sack immediately. It came from the lingerie shop where she and Breanna had looked at the bra and thong yesterday. "You didn't."

"I did. I knew you wouldn't buy that gorgeous underwear, so I did it for you."

"Bre..."

"Don't 'Bre' me, Mom." She passed the sack to her mother. "Try them on. I want to see how sexy you are in them."

"I take back what I said about raising a smart girl. I raised a brat instead."

Breanna grinned. "You're so lucky." She waved a hand toward her mother. "No stalling. I want to be sure they fit."

Jade opened the sack and removed the emerald bra and thong. They felt as light as air in her hands. Her heart beat a bit faster at the thought of wearing something so sexy. She liked pretty lingerie, but never wore anything as skimpy as these.

"Mom? Aren't you going to try them on?"

Sighing heavily, Jade let the underwear drop to her lap. "I can't wear these, Bre."

"Why not?"

"Because I'm not..." She gestured at the silky lingerie. "I'm not the type of woman who wears this kind of...stuff."

"Again I ask, why not? And don't give me that bullshit about you being forty in two weeks."

"I *will* be forty in two weeks."

"So does that mean you stop being a woman, or feeling desire? You love reading erotic romances. Don't they affect you? Don't the love scenes turn you on?"

"Well, yes, sometimes—"

"Don't you fantasize about making love with a man, having him touch you?"

Warmth crept into Jade's face. Breanna would probably be mortified to know how many times her mother fantasized about being intimate with a man, and all the different *ways* of being intimate...especially the anal sex fantasies. Jade cleared her throat. "Breanna, I think we're getting a bit too personal."

"Why?" Breanna moved closer and laid her hand over Jade's. "You've always told me I could talk to you about anything. That goes both ways. I'm not simply being a daughter who loves her mother when I tell you how special and lovely you are. You're surrounded by men because of your job. There's no reason why you can't find a man who will *adore* you. Why won't you give anyone a chance?"

Jade pushed her hair behind her right ear. "When your husband leaves you for a younger woman, it doesn't exactly boost up your self-esteem."

Breanna remained silent for several seconds before softly saying, "No, I guess it doesn't. But that was two years ago, Mom. Let it go."

"I've tried, Bre. I really have tried to let it go." Lowering her gaze to the lingerie in her lap, Jade fingered the silky material. "I thought we had a good marriage. I thought I'd made your father happy, in every way. That included the bedroom."

Breanna squeezed Jade's hand, but didn't speak.

"We had a good sex life. Let me rephrase that—*I* had a good sex life. Apparently your father didn't."

"It wasn't just sex, Mom. I think it was more of an ego thing for Dad. He's very dominant. I don't mean in a sexual way. At least, I don't think you two had that kind of relationship, and I certainly don't want you to tell me. That would be way too much information. But you aren't a fawner and Melody was. He needed someone to hang on his every word and jump at his slightest command."

Jade looked back at her daughter. "You're using past tense phrases, Bre."

"I know. Dad and Melody broke up three weeks ago."

Perhaps the news should've been more of a shock to Jade, but it wasn't. She'd never believed Carl and Melody would last forever. The fact that they never married proved that. "I didn't know."

Breanna shrugged. "I didn't think it would make any difference to you. It's not as if you and Dad will ever get back together." Her eyes widened and a look of panic filled them. "You won't, will you?"

Jade couldn't help laughing at her daughter's stricken expression. "I thought all children wanted their divorced parents to get back together."

"Not me. I've watched you grow into your own person since you and Dad split. He's too domineering for you, Mom. You need an equal, someone who will love you for the person you are, not the person he wants you to be. You need a guy who will appreciate you and love you so much, he'd never consider even *looking* at another woman, much less take her to bed."

"Men like that don't exist in my age bracket."

"Who says he has to be in your age bracket? How about someone younger than you, someone handsome with a great body and a huge cock who'll make you come three times a night?"

Jade's mouth dropped open at her daughter's language. "Breanna!"

She grinned. "Nice fantasy, isn't it?"

Jade returned her daughter's grin. "It certainly is."

Breanna giggled. "Well, I don't want a guy younger than me, but the rest of it would work." She pointed to the lingerie in her mother's lap. "And speaking of a younger man, you have a date in a few hours. Try on your new undies."

"You're determined for me to wear these, aren't you?"

"Absolutely. So up! Try them on."

Arguing would be useless, Jade knew that. She could humor her daughter by trying on the underwear. That didn't mean she had to wear it tonight.

"And don't think you can get away with trying them on now and not wearing them tonight. I'll be back to check on you later."

"I hate it when you read my mind." With a sigh of defeat, Jade climbed off the bed. "I can't believe I'm doing this."

"It's a day for firsts. Believe me, it was a first for me to buy a bra with a double D cup."

Modesty had never been a problem for Jade with her daughter. She had taught Breanna that the human body was beautiful, not something "dirty", no matter the shape or size. Peeling off her T-shirt, jeans, and underwear, she let them fall to the floor.

"God, Mom, you have a better body than some of my girlfriends. You don't have one tiny bit of cellulite anywhere. I think I hate you." Breanna stretched out on the bed and rested on one elbow. "I don't know why you think you need to lose thirty pounds."

"My scale makes me think that."

"You should throw away that stupid scale and simply use your mirror."

Jade slipped on the bra first. It didn't have any padding, but the style pushed her breasts together and upward, creating a deep cleavage. She eyed the thong as if it would morph into a rattlesnake at any moment before taking a breath and stepping into it. After arranging the elastic so it was comfortable, she faced her daughter, hands on hips.

"Well?"

Breanna grinned. "You're a total babe. Go look at yourself in the mirror."

Jade crossed the floor and stopped in front of the three-way mirror. She turned left, then right, examining her body from every angle. A frown formed on her lips. This wasn't her. She liked nice lingerie, yes, but not a bra that made her breasts look even larger, and definitely not a thong that barely covered her pubic hair.

"Don't look at *you*, Mom. Look at the woman in the mirror. See how sexy she is."

Jade met her daughter's gaze in the glass before shifting her attention back to her own image. She turned from side to side again so she could see her entire body. The woman in the mirror looked…voluptuous, sexy, confident of her appeal to men.

Totally different from the chubby divorcee she usually saw in the mirror.

"If that was a friend of yours, would you think she looked good? Be honest."

Honestly, yes, she looked good. A tiny smile played across her lips. She looked *damned* good.

"You'll have that escort drooling all over you."

"He's paid to drool over me." She met Breanna's gaze in the mirror again. "By the way, how much *did* you pay him?"

"That's none of your business."

"*That* much? Breanna, the trust fund from your grandfather wasn't meant to be blown on foolish things."

"I'm not blowing my trust fund, Mom, I promise. You don't worry about the cost. The only thing you have to worry about tonight is having a good time."

"And making sure everything runs smoothly."

"It will. You're incredible at your job and everything always runs exactly the way it's supposed to."

Jade smiled. "Thanks, honey. You're good for my ego." She turned and walked back to the bed. "I have an idea."

"What?"

"I'll get dressed and we'll go out for an early lunch. I'll buy."

"You bet you will. I'm tapped out after paying for your rent-a-stud."

Chapter Three

ꕥ

Breanna sighed heavily when Jade tried again to pull up the bodice of her gown. "Mom, stop that. You're going to tear it."

"Are you sure this isn't too low?"

"No, it isn't too low." Breanna pushed away Jade's hands and tugged the bodice back down to where it should be. "You have beautiful breasts. Don't be afraid to show them off. I'd show mine off every opportunity I got if they were as big as yours."

"Are you sure my nipples are covered?"

"Yes, Mom, they're covered." She grinned. "Barely."

Ignoring her mother's glare, Breanna straightened the sweetheart neckline, then took a step back to look at Jade. She looked absolutely stunning. The long-sleeved emerald gown had definitely been the right choice. It made her mother's eyes appear an even deeper green, her hair a richer shade of auburn. While not tight, the silky material clung to Jade's curves, emphasizing her breasts and hips.

That sexy escort wouldn't be able to breathe when he saw Jade. And that's exactly what Breanna wanted. She wanted her mother to have a good time tonight, both at the gala and later in the bedroom.

"You realize I never wear anything like this," Jade said. "My gowns are more—"

"Boring," Breanna quickly supplied.

"Sedate. I represent the hospital, Bre. I have to look professional."

"You look professional every day at work. This is a party. You're allowed to let loose and be sexy."

"I doubt if the board would approve of my having a good time if it means my nipples pop out of my bodice."

Breanna swallowed her smile. Her mother had a quick wit and a terrific sense of humor. Any man would enjoy being with her because of her sparkling personality. Although with Jade's looks and body, Breanna doubted if he would pass up the opportunity to be with her physically, too.

Including the escort. *Especially* the escort. Breanna had made sure of that.

Jade laid one hand over her stomach. "I swear there are five thousand butterflies in here."

"I'll get you a glass of tea."

"Thanks, honey."

Breanna left Jade in the bedroom while she walked to the kitchen. She thought back to earlier today and her conversation with Zachary Cooper. Wanting to be sure he knew exactly what she expected of him, she'd called Coopers' Companions this morning and asked for Zach to call her cell. She'd been in the bookstore when he'd returned her call.

"Ms. Talmage, this is Zachary Cooper. How can I help you?"

Breanna shivered hearing that deep, sexy voice. Oh, yes, he would be perfect for her mother. "Thank you for calling me, Mr. Cooper."

"Zach, please."

"And I'm Breanna." She stepped to a corner of the store for more privacy. "I wanted to make sure you understand about tonight."

"I'm escorting your mother to the gala celebrating the one-hundredth anniversary of North Texas Highland Hospital."

"I'm not talking about the gala. I'm talking about *after* the gala."

"I don't understand."

Breanna glanced around to be sure no one stood close enough to hear her. "I want my mother to have a good time tonight. That includes sex."

He remained silent for several seconds. "Did your mother ask you to call me?"

"No. She'd shoot me if she knew I was doing this."

"Ms. Talmage—Breanna—it is totally up to the woman if our evening ends with a more…intimate encounter. It isn't Coopers' Companions' policy to come on to the woman we're escorting."

"But your dates do include sex. My girlfriend, the one who recommended you, said her date with you ended with sex."

Intense, mind-blowing sex. Breanna shivered again. She'd had sex, but never intense, mind-blowing sex. It sounded nummy.

"I'm not sure if this conversation is appropriate, Ms. Talmage."

"No, it probably isn't, but I'm concerned about my mother. I want her to feel…sexy and alive. I want *you* to make her feel that way." She paused a moment as a customer walked past. "So, will your evening with my mother include sex?"

"Ms. Talmage, I am an escort, a companion. I am not a prostitute."

"I didn't say you are. But we're both adults, Zach. Be honest with me. Many of your dates end with sex, don't they?"

She heard him sigh. "If the lady requests it, yes. My job is to be attentive to my date, to show her she's appreciated because she's a woman."

"What if she doesn't request sex?"

"Then I say goodnight at her front door and go home."

Breanna blew out a heavy breath. "My mother won't request it. I want you to initiate sex."

"I will not do anything to make your mother uncomfortable."

She couldn't let him slip away. Frantically thinking about a way to get through to him, she said the first thing that popped into her head. "I'll give you more money—"

"Money is not the issue. I will escort your mother to the gala. I will be attentive and gracious to her. I will not initiate sex if she doesn't want it."

Well, shit. Now what?

"It's been a long time for her. She hasn't been intimate with anyone since she and my dad divorced almost two years ago. I know that for a fact because she told me so. My mother is a young, beautiful, sexy woman, Zach. She's been alone much too long. I want her to feel desirable again."

"I'm sorry. Unless your mother indicates she wants to be intimate with me, it won't happen."

"But if you get any kind of sign from her, any little thing, you'll go for it?"

Zach chuckled. "You're very persistent, Breanna."

She took his chuckling as a good sign. "I'm a lot like my mother."

When he didn't say anything else, Breanna prompted him. "Any little sign, right?"

"Yes, any little sign."

"All right!" If she wasn't in a bookstore, she would've done a happy dance. "Show her a good time. And I mean a *really* good time. You'll spend the night with her, right?"

"No. You won't change my mind about that. We don't spend the night with our dates. Ever."

"But you can stay with her for a long time, right? I mean, the gala won't even be over until probably midnight."

"Staying late won't be a problem."

Breanna beamed. "Wonderful. Thank you, Zach."

Yes, her mother would shoot her if she knew Breanna had called Zach. But she had to be sure that he paid extra special attention to Jade tonight.

She poured each of them a glass of iced tea and returned to the bedroom. She found her mother in the bathroom, putting the final touches on her hair. "Here, Mom."

"Thanks, Bre." Jade accepted the glass. She chugged down half the contents in one gulp.

"You really are nervous, aren't you?"

"I'm going out with a man I don't know, a man I've never even *seen*. I've never had a blind date. Of *course* I'm nervous." She took another sip of tea before placing the glass on the counter. "What a stupid time for my brother to go on a fishing trip."

"I think Uncle Paul purposely planned his trip when he did so he wouldn't have to escort you. He hates wearing a tux."

"'Escort'. There's that word again. Do you know *anything* about him, Bre?"

I know he's going to give you the best sex of your life. No offense, Dad. "Not a thing." Picking up Jade's brush, Breanna smoothed an errant curl by her mother's left ear. "Stop worrying. Everything will be fine. The gala will go smoothly, and you'll have a wonderful time."

The sound of a car pulling into the driveway made Breanna toss down the brush and jog to the window. She pulled apart two slats of the mini-blinds and peered outside. The sight made her gasp.

"What?" Jade asked anxiously.

"He's driving a Lexus. What a sweet car."

"Do you see him?"

"Not really. He's... Wait, he's getting out." Breanna swallowed hard. Her knees trembled. Her knees *never* trembled at the sight of a handsome man. But rarely did she see a man so totally edible. "Oh my God. Mom, he's *gorgeous*!"

Jade joined Breanna at the window. "He's a *baby*!"

"Oooh, *baby*!"

"Breanna, I cannot go to the gala with a man that young. He can't be more than twenty-five."

"He's thirty."

Jade took Breanna's arm and pulled her away from the window. "I thought you didn't know anything about him."

Oops. Watch it, Bre. "I don't, other than his age. But what difference does that make?"

"I do not want to go out with a man ten years younger!"

The doorbell rang. "It's too late to back out now, Mom."

Jade huffed out a breath. Her eyes narrowed. "I *am* going to spank you for this."

She turned as if to leave the room. Breanna quickly grabbed her arm to stop her.

"Uh-uh. I'll answer the door. You need to make an entrance."

"An entrance?"

"Yeah. Wait two minutes."

Breanna hurried from the bathroom while her mom hissed at her to come back. She wanted Zach to watch her mother walk down the hall. She wanted him to see the gentle jiggle of Jade's breasts above her bodice and realize that beautiful woman would be in his arms tonight.

Besides, she wanted a close-up view of him first.

She opened the front door as the chimes sounded a second time. Her mouth would've dropped open if she hadn't caught it in time. She didn't know if Zachary Cooper was the most handsome man she'd ever seen, but he had to be in the top ten.

The top five.

Tall, at least six-one. Medium brown, shoulder-length hair with a hint of curl. Impossibly broad shoulders. Wide chest. Flat stomach. Husky thighs. A nice bulge between those thighs.

A *very* nice bulge.

Breanna sighed silently. Oh, yes, he would do quite nicely.

"Hi," Breanna said when she managed to find her voice again.

He smiled. "Good evening."

"Come in, please. I'm Breanna. My mom will be ready in a minute."

She shut the door behind Zach. When she faced him again, he took her hand, lifted it to his mouth, and placed a soft kiss on the back.

"It's a pleasure to meet you, Breanna."

Her breath hitched. "Oh, you're good," she whispered.

"I know," he whispered back with a grin.

He straightened and released her hand. She saw his gaze flick past her shoulder. The amusement in his expression quickly faded, to be replaced with an emotion she'd call awe.

Which quickly turned into downright lust.

Breanna turned and watched her mother gliding toward them. That's the best word she could think of to describe the way Jade moved…almost as if her feet didn't touch the floor. Tears filled her eyes. She was so proud of her stunning mother.

"Good evening," Jade said softly once she stood before Zach.

He cleared his throat. "Good evening. I'm Zachary Cooper, your escort for tonight." He held out a single white rose to her.

She gave him a small smile. "Jade Talmage." She held out her free hand to him. Instead of shaking it, he took it in both of his and lifted it to his mouth. He kissed the back, then her palm.

Breanna sighed. How romantic.

When neither of them moved for a full fifteen seconds, Breanna clasped their arms and ushered them toward the door. "You two have a good time. Mom, I'll lock up and put the rose in water. Zach, nice to meet you. Bye."

She plucked the rose from Jade's fingers and practically slammed the door in their faces. Grinning, she headed back down the hall to Jade's bedroom. She had a few more items hidden in her bookstore bag that she planned to leave for her mother to find…items to make the evening even hotter.

Chapter Four

ꙮ

Zach had forgotten to breathe when he saw Jade walk down the hall toward him. He'd seen hundreds of beautiful women. He'd been intimate with dozens. Why one woman would affect him so strongly, he didn't know.

He had to find out.

Placing his hand lightly on Jade's lower back, he steered her toward the passenger side of his car. "You look beautiful, Jade."

"Thank you."

That voice. Soft, sensual, made to stir a man's desires with nothing more than a whisper.

He imagined that voice begging him to fuck her as he pounded his cock into her tight, wet pussy.

Opening the door, he held her hand as she slid onto the seat. The slit in her dress blessed him with a glimpse of her right leg to just above her knee before she quickly closed it. He saw a shapely leg covered by a silky stocking. Somehow, he knew she wasn't wearing pantyhose. Perhaps a garter belt, or those lace-topped, thigh-high stockings that stayed up by themselves.

Wondering would keep his cock half hard all evening.

He meant what he'd told Breanna earlier today on the phone—it was not Coopers' Companions' policy to come on to their dates. Zach had always lived by that rule and had never been tempted to break it.

Jade tempted him.

Why? What is it about this woman that affects me so much?

Zach shut Jade's door and walked around the front of the car to the driver's side. Once behind the wheel, he looked at her. She glanced at him, but her gaze quickly skittered away again.

His heart did a funny jog in his chest.

Silently, Zach backed out of the driveway. He drove two blocks before he pushed a CD into the player. Soft saxophone music filled the car.

"Music okay?" he asked.

"It's nice."

"You like the sax?"

"Very much."

He glanced her way as he slowed at a yield sign. "Do you like to dance?"

"I do, but I'm not very good."

"I have trouble believing that."

"You'd believe it in about five seconds. That's how long it would take me to step on your foot."

Zach chuckled. He liked her sense of humor, and her honesty. "Will there be dancing tonight?"

"Yes."

He looked at her again, longer this time. He could hardly wait to hold her in his arms. "I'll take my chances."

Jade shifted in her seat so she could see him better. The dim glow from the dash gave her enough light to easily make out his features. Bre hadn't been exaggerating when she called him gorgeous. His medium brown hair brushed his shoulders. She'd never been partial to long hair on a man, but she had to admit Zach's hair was very sexy. She wondered if it felt as soft as it looked. Straight nose, strong chin with a hint of cleft, square jaw, full lips…they all combined to make him positively yummy.

Jade had always had a weakness for blue eyes. Zach's were the color of a cloudless sky an hour before sunset. One look from those intense blue eyes would make a woman vow to do his every bidding.

Her gaze slowly traveled over his body. He wore a tuxedo as if he were born for it. His jacket hung open, giving her an unobstructed view of his body. She admired the wide chest and flat stomach. She especially admired the healthy bulge between his thighs that not even the perfect cut of his trousers could hide.

Jade couldn't help the small sigh that escaped her lips. Such masculine beauty. Too bad she could enjoy it for only a few hours.

But for those few hours, she *would* enjoy it.

She'd made the decision as soon as she slid into his car. Knowing a man ten years her junior would be her escort for the evening had made her feel…wicked. She'd immediately worried what her coworkers at the hospital would think when she walked into the gala on Zach's arm. Then she decided she didn't care. He was a handsome, sexy man who'd been hired to be her companion for the evening. She had every right to enjoy herself…and him.

That didn't mean sex, of course. She had no intention of being intimate with a man who'd had sex with who knew how many women.

Even though it would be so nice to feel a man's hands touching her again, his lips on hers, his tongue darting into her mouth, his hard cock sliding into her wet pussy…

A jolt zinged through her clit. Two years of celibacy was a long time. She missed that closeness, that intimacy, with a man.

He turned down the volume on the CD player. "Is this the first time you've hired an escort?"

"I didn't hire you, my daughter did."

"So it *is* the first time?"

"Yes. My brother usually escorts me, but he's in Florida on a deep-sea fishing trip."

"Are you uncomfortable having me for your escort?"

"I was, at first."

"No more?"

Jade had always believed honesty to be important. Although she barely knew Zach, she saw no reason to change that belief. "You're a very handsome, sexy man, Zach. I'm going to enjoy being with you tonight."

He glanced her way and smiled. "Good."

Realizing how that could have sounded, Jade quickly continued. "I didn't mean I'm going to *be* with you. I meant at the gala. I'm going to enjoy your company at the gala."

"I knew what you meant, Jade."

"Oh." Heat filled her cheeks. Of course he knew what she'd meant. Just because she felt attracted to him didn't mean he felt the same way. Why should he? She was ten years his senior. The women he usually dated were probably his age or younger—women who had firm bodies with smaller breasts that hadn't been affected by gravity yet.

He expertly handled the luxury car over the side streets heading toward downtown Fort Worth. The car, the tuxedo, his mannerisms, screamed money. Apparently he made a very good income as an escort. Jade couldn't help but wonder how he'd gotten into this type of business in the first place. "Have you done this for a long time?"

"Done what?"

"Escorted women."

"About ten years."

It surprised her to hear he'd started as a rent-a-stud so young. "You were twenty?"

"Twenty-one." He stopped at a red light before looking at her. "How do you know my age?"

"Breanna told me."

Zach didn't say anything for several moments. "Does my age bother you? It shouldn't. Age is a number. It's no indication of who you are as a person."

"That's easy for a thirty-year-old to say. It's a bit different for a woman pushing forty."

His gaze passed over her hair, her face, her breasts, before he looked into her eyes again. "You're a lovely woman, Jade. You'll be lovely no matter your age."

A warm glow filled her at his compliment. He certainly knew all the right words to say. But he *should* know all the right words after ten years of practice.

Realizing he'd probably used those same words on countless other women deflated her attraction a bit.

Face it, Jade. Whatever he says to you is memorized. He's the same as an actor, and has been for ten years. He'll say whatever he thinks a woman wants to hear.

The light turned green and Zach passed through the intersection. He'd paid compliments to other women, even when they weren't true. It was his job to make his date feel special, and sometimes that included some exaggeration. He'd never felt guilty about "fudging" a little. As long as he made his date feel good about herself, that's all that mattered to him.

He meant every word he said to Jade. Somehow, he had to convince her of his sincerity.

Another red light gave him the opportunity to face her again. "All women are beautiful, Jade. Some are more physically appealing than others, but each woman is special in her own way. She becomes even more special as she ages. I truly meant what I said about age being a number. Yes, it's a cliché, but it's true." He draped his left wrist over the steering wheel. "You'll be forty soon?"

Jade nodded. "On May 13."

"Does turning forty bother you?"

"No. Getting older is better than the alternative."

"That's true."

"There's another cliché about life beginning at forty. I guess I'll find out in a couple of weeks."

"Are you where you want to be? Job, home, family, that kind of thing."

"In some things, yes. In others, no."

"What's missing in your life?"

A sharp beep from the car behind him startled Zach. He'd been so focused on Jade, he hadn't noticed when the light changed to green. Pressing on the gas pedal, he drove through the intersection.

He noticed she didn't answer his question.

The hotel where the gala would be held sat on the next block, so Zach didn't have the chance to question Jade further. He assumed her marriage was one of those things that hadn't worked out the way she wanted. No one got married with plans of getting a divorce.

He wondered if she still loved her ex-husband.

He followed Jade's directions to the parking garage. After traveling up three levels, he found a parking space within ten yards of the elevator.

"How often do you get a parking place so close to the entrance?" he said after putting the gearshift into Park. "My luck is good tonight."

"You haven't danced with me yet."

"You're still determined you're going to step on my foot?"

Jade raised one hand, palm toward him. "I so solemnly swear."

Zach chuckled. The more time he spent with Jade, the more he liked her. He couldn't remember ever feeling such a strong connection with a woman. "I'm still willing to take my chances. After all, dancing will give me the chance to hold you in my arms."

He watched her gaze roam over his face as she bit her bottom lip. He waited for her to speak. When she remained silent for several moments, Zach spoke. "Is something wrong?"

"No. I was just…thinking."

"About what?" he asked softly.

"Nothing important."

Reaching over, he lightly touched the back of her left hand. "You can talk to me, Jade. I'm a great listener."

Jade looked down at their hands—his tan, hers much lighter. It seemed…natural for him to touch her. She didn't like that. She didn't like feeling this attraction for a man who paid compliments to women for money. He could call himself an escort, a companion. No matter what name he used, he was still a rent-a-stud.

"We'd better go in," she said, sliding her hand from beneath his.

By the time Jade had gathered up her purse and wrap, Zach had rounded the car and opened her door. He held out his hand to her. It would be rude of her not to accept it. Placing her hand in his, she let him help her from the car.

Once standing, she was trapped between the car's door frame and Zach's body. A zing sizzled through her clit again when she looked up into his eyes. She wanted to be in his arms, and not just on the dance floor.

That would *not* happen. She wouldn't be the next in a long line of his conquests.

"Are you sure there's nothing wrong?" he asked. "You…pulled away from me."

"You're my escort, Zach, that's all. I won't fall for your practiced lines of seduction."

He frowned. "'Practiced lines of seduction'? Where did *that* come from?"

"After ten years, I'm sure you know all the words to say to make a woman melt at your feet. Well, I won't. I want that clear from the start. You're my escort to a business function. That's all."

His eyes narrowed and anger flared through them. He lowered his gaze for a moment. When he looked at her again, the anger had disappeared. Now she saw no emotion at all.

Zach held out his arm to her. "Shall we go in, Ms. Talmage?"

Chin high, Jade cupped her hand around the bend of his elbow. Silently, he directed her toward the elevator.

Chapter Five

ஐ

Zach behaved like the perfect gentleman. Jade couldn't find fault in anything he did. He took her wrap to check when they entered the ballroom. He asked her if she wanted a drink, and headed to the bar to get the glass of red wine she requested. He smiled often, said all the right phrases, made small talk with the people who came up to speak to her.

She hated every moment of it.

The Zach in the car had been funny, charming, flirtatious. He'd made her feel comfortable and eager to spend more time with him. This man was a rent-a-stud.

Jade endured it for twenty minutes before she couldn't stand being near the mannequin Zach had become. Unfortunately, the head of surgery and his wife had cornered them and Jade didn't know how to gracefully get away from them. Doctor Douglas Lassiter loved to talk, and his wife, Marianne, loved to talk even more.

"You should see it, Jade," Marianne gushed. "Doug designed it himself and had it built while we were on our cruise. It's *huge*. Crystal water, live plants, rock formations." She shuddered and sighed. Jade wondered if she'd had an orgasm. "It's almost a shame to swim in it."

"It sounds lovely," Jade said politely. *I don't care about your new swimming pool, or your remodeled master bedroom, or the 1,968 pairs of shoes you probably own.*

"Oh, and the *gazebo*!" Marianne gripped Jade's wrist. Jade had to catch herself before she winced from those long, manicured fingernails. "Doug had it enlarged. It's *gorgeous*."

Is there anything you have that isn't gorgeous? "I'm sure you'll enjoy it." *How can I get away from you when you're digging your claws into my skin?*

Zach took the problem out of her hands. "Dr. Lassiter, Mrs. Lassiter, would you please excuse us? I see someone I'd like Jade to meet."

"Of course," Doug said. "Jade, we'll see you later. We're seated at your table."

She'd forgotten about that. It was incredibly stupid of her to seat Doug and Marianne at the same table as she and Zach.

Jade forced herself to give Doug a bright smile. "Wonderful. We'll see you at dinner."

Placing his hand lightly under her left elbow, Zach led her away from the couple. "You owe me for that one."

Jade chuckled. "Yes, I do. Thank you."

"Just doing my job."

His angry tone of voice made her stop and look at him. He returned her look, his eyes cool. "I don't like that."

"You don't like what?"

"That reference to your job."

"Isn't that what you wanted? You informed me in the garage I'm nothing but your escort, that you won't fall for any practiced lines of seduction."

Her words thrown back at her sounded so cruel. He turned his head, but not before she saw the flash of irritation in his eyes. She didn't know if she'd hurt him or simply bruised his ego. Either instance warranted an apology.

"I didn't intentionally mean to be so rude."

Jade saw his chest rise and fall with a deep breath. His eyes were no longer cool when he looked back at her, but still flat. "Apology accepted."

"Shall we start over?"

He squeezed her elbow. "An excellent idea." A hint of warmth returned to his eyes. "Hi, Jade, I'm Zach. I'll be your escort this evening."

Jade smiled. She liked this Zach much better.

"Would you like another glass of wine?" he asked.

"Yes, but I'll go with you to the bar this time."

"You're afraid Marianne Lassiter will hunt you down again."

"You're right about that."

"Well, then, my lady, I give you my protection." He offered her his arm. "Shall we?"

She wrapped her hand around his biceps. "We shall."

* * * * *

Zach watched Jade work the room. She spoke to everyone who called to her, handled several last-minute problems with someone's special food order or the seating arrangement. Instead of calling on one of the staff to do it, she personally moved two flower arrangements on the tables because someone was allergic to roses.

She fascinated him.

Leaning back in his chair, Zach took a sip of his iced tea. He didn't drink when he had to drive, nor on a date. He could better judge what his companion desired when alcohol didn't make his head fuzzy.

He wanted to be clearheaded so he knew *exactly* what Jade desired.

He'd meant it when he'd told Breanna that it would be up to Jade whether or not the evening ended with him in Jade's bed. He'd never pushed a woman for sex. He didn't have to. Women did salivate at the sight of him. That knowledge could easily inflate his ego. Knowing he really wasn't God's gift to women helped keep him focused.

He loved sex. That moment when he slid his hard cock inside a woman's creamy pussy, that instant of resistance before her body accepted him…nothing felt better. He craved sex, and he craved it often. Yet if a woman simply wanted an escort and not sex, no problem. It was completely up to her. It would be the same tonight with Jade.

Despite her adamant refusal to accept him as anything more than an escort, he couldn't help hoping she would want to make love with him tonight.

She carried herself with confidence…head up, back straight, those luscious breasts thrust forward. She was a woman who knew what she wanted and wouldn't take anything less. He admired that.

Her ex-husband had to be crazy to let her go.

Zach set his glass on the table. He wanted her. The small amount of time he'd spent with her wasn't nearly enough. He longed to hold her, touch her, feel her skin sliding against his, hear her breath catch when she came…

The sudden thickening of his cock made him shift in his chair. He hadn't been with a woman for three weeks, and the part of his anatomy with a mind of its own didn't hesitate to remind him of that fact. But it wasn't simply the lack of sex that made him react to Jade. In the past, he'd gone for several weeks without a woman when working on a house took up all his time and zapped his energy. He wanted Jade because of Jade and no other reason.

She turned her head his direction. He dipped his chin to acknowledge her, and she gave him a small smile. Turning back to the people standing with her, she spoke for another moment before walking toward him.

He had time to thoroughly admire her voluptuous body in the clinging emerald gown before she reached her chair.

He stood and held the chair for her while she slipped into it, then returned to his own chair, pulling it a bit closer to hers.

"Through schmoozing?" he asked.

"For now." She waved her hand in front of her face. "Is it warm in here, or is it just me?"

"You've been busy."

"Unfortunately, yes. I'm sorry I've been ignoring you."

"Don't be. You have a job to do. I understand that. You told me you'd be with me in fifteen minutes." He pushed back his left cuff and looked at his watch. "Right on time."

Jade chuckled. "Breanna would be proud of me. She's always on my case about being late."

"She's a lovely young lady."

"Thank you. I could brag about her for hours, but I don't want to bore you."

"Listening to a mother talk about the daughter she loves would never be boring."

He watched Jade's gaze travel over his face, as if trying to decide whether or not to believe him. "Do you always know the right thing to say?"

Zach could pop off a practiced answer. He knew enough of them to spout them all evening. With Jade, he wanted only honesty. "No," he said softly, "I don't always know the right thing to say."

"You seem to."

"Is that a polite way of implying I have a dictionary of phrases in my head?"

A couple slid into their chairs directly across the table before Jade said anything else. Zach muttered a curse at the interruption. It bothered him to think Jade might believe him to be nothing more than a professional charmer with a dick for hire.

Isn't that what you are, Cooper?

Telling the voice in his head to mind its own business, Zach smiled politely at the couple just seated before facing Jade again. "Would you like another glass of wine?"

She glanced at his iced tea. "Actually, I was thinking of stealing your tea."

Zach picked up his glass and presented it to Jade. "Help yourself. I'll get another one when the waiter comes by."

She hesitated a moment, then accepted his glass. He watched her take a long sip.

Directly on the spot where his lips had been.

His cock surged to life. Any little sign, Breanna had said. Any little sign that showed him Jade wanted to be intimate. He could take that as a sign, or he could realize she didn't know she'd drunk from the same spot as he.

Her gaze met his as she drank again. *She knows,* Zach thought. *She knows* exactly *what she's doing.*

Zach smiled to himself. *Why, you little temptress.* Leaning back in his chair, he laid his left arm on the back of Jade's chair. He touched the bare skin above her gown with his thumb. He watched her face as he circled his thumb over her satiny skin. She closed her eyes briefly before looking at him again. Desire clearly showed in her eyes.

She wants me as much as I want her.

He'd love to grab her hand, yank her from her chair, and drag her to some dark corner where no one would see them. He'd pull up her gown to her waist, free his aching cock, and drive inside that sweet pussy. Over and over, he'd pound into her while she clutched his shoulders and moaned into his ear. Once wouldn't be enough. As soon as she came, he'd start fucking her again…and again…and again…

"Hello again, Jade."

Doug Lassiter slid into the chair next to Jade, putting an end to Zach's fantasy. Jade released a breath and turned to the man sitting at her left. "Hello."

Marianne joined her husband. "I *do* hope the *food* is good. I'm absolutely *famished*."

Zach sensed the tension in Jade's body. She was in charge of this entire gala, which meant she'd decided on the menu. Marianne's implication that the food might not be good had to be a direct dig to Jade. He started to say something to take up for her, but Jade beat him to it.

"The chefs here are excellent, Marianne. I'm sure you'll find the food delicious."

"It isn't *chicken*, is it? Every time we *attend* one of these *things*, they serve us *chicken*."

"No, it isn't chicken. We're having prime rib."

"Oh. *Oh*! Well, that *does* sound delicious, and a *welcome* change."

Zach cleared his throat to hide his chuckle. He wondered if Marianne Lassiter always emphasized every other word she spoke.

His little temptress had claws. He liked that.

Jade leaned toward him. Zach moved closer and lowered his head so she could speak without being heard. "Stop that," she whispered into his ear.

"Stop what?" he whispered back.

"Stop touching me."

He tilted his head so he could see her face, a mere six inches from his own. "Why?"

"Because it makes me *crazy*."

Zach grinned. "Good crazy or bad crazy?"

"All right, you two, knock it off," Doug said playfully. "No flirting at the table."

"I think it's sweet," Marianne said. She propped her elbows on the table and laced her fingers together beneath her chin. "Although I can't help wondering why we haven't met you before tonight, Zach. Where has Jade been *hiding* you?"

Not exactly subtle, are you, Mrs. Lassiter? Zach leaned back in his chair again. That eager look in Marianne's eyes told him she wanted all the dirt on Jade's new beau. He could tell her the truth, without telling her the *whole* truth. "We haven't known each other very long."

"What do you do for a living?"

"I build houses."

If he hadn't still been touching Jade, he wouldn't have noticed her slight jump of surprise. She knew nothing of his other job for he hadn't had the chance to tell her yet.

"You're in construction?" Doug asked.

Zach nodded. "My uncle owns a construction firm here in Fort Worth. I help him off and on, whenever he's short a worker. Right now, I'm working on my own, building my house."

"You're very...*young* to be building a house all by yourself."

Marianne didn't fool him for a moment. He knew she meant he was too young for Jade. Her implication made Zach see red. Outwardly, he remained calm and polite. "Age has nothing to do with talent, don't you agree?"

He purposely wrapped his hand around Jade's nape so Marianne could see it. Her eyes narrowed as she followed the track of his fingers caressing Jade's neck.

"Well, yes," she said. "I suppose you're right. Still—"

"Marianne, leave them alone." Doug's voice sounded controlled, yet Zach heard the steel beneath the words. He faced them and smiled. “My wife has to know everything about everyone she meets.”

“I’m only being friendly, Doug.”

“You’re being nosy, as usual.”

Marianne huffed and picked up her glass of water. Zach exchanged a look with Jade. She managed to keep a straight face, but he could see the humor in her eyes.

He also saw her eyes cross when he slid his thumb up to her ear and caressed the lobe.

Other couples began to filter to their table, as did the waiters. Zach gave Jade’s nape a gentle squeeze before he released it. *Later,* he mouthed.

He saw her throat work as she swallowed.

Chapter Six

ཉ

Jade clapped when Dr. Jennings, the hospital's administrator, finished his speech, even though it had to be the most boring speech she'd ever heard. The man ran the hospital beautifully, but he had zero personality.

"A bit of a dud, huh?" Zach whispered in her ear.

His warm breath sent a shiver racing down her spine. Shivers had been racing up and down her spine all evening. A simple look from Zach's incredible blue eyes made her stomach quiver and her nipples bead.

She didn't want to want him.

Jade could fight her own body's desires and she would. Having sex with Zach would probably feel good. Even mechanical sex would feel good after two years of celibacy.

Somehow, she knew nothing about sex with Zach would be the least bit mechanical.

Even though her body wanted to, it would be incredibly stupid. There could be no future for them. If she had sex with him, it would be nothing more than a one-night stand.

So what's wrong with that?

That little voice in her head sounded suspiciously like Breanna.

"Now that I've completely bored all of you," the administrator said, grinning when he received several chuckles and light applause, "it's time for some fun. Dancing in the next room."

"Ah, finally," Zach said. "Ready to step on my foot?"

"You're a glutton for punishment, aren't you?"

Jade allowed Zach to take her hand and help her from her chair. He didn't release her hand once they stood, but held it all the way to the dance floor. His palm felt warm and slightly rough against hers. She assumed the roughness came from calluses since he worked in construction.

A five-piece band played "How Can You Mend a Broken Heart". Zach drew her into his arms. Jade laid her left hand on his shoulder, her fingers inches from his hair. He tugged her a bit closer to him, until her breasts brushed his chest. It felt so good in his arms, so right, as if they'd danced together before tonight.

Zach smiled at her. "So far, so good. My feet are unbruised."

"It's only our first dance."

"I like to live dangerously."

He did a fast spin and dipped her. Jade laughed at his silliness. Feeling a bit lightheaded after he raised her upright again, she clutched his shoulder tighter. "Making me dizzy isn't a good idea. Your feet will suffer."

"I think you're teasing me about stepping on my feet. You're very graceful."

His gaze swept over her face, her hair. It dipped briefly to her cleavage, making her catch her breath. When he looked at her face again, she could clearly see the heat in his eyes.

Her heart fluttered in her chest.

He'd been with dozens of women, perhaps even scores. He knew all the moves, all the right things to say. She had trouble believing, even with all his experience, that he could fake desire.

"Are you having a good time?" he asked.

"Yes. You're a wonderful dancer."

"This is nothing. You should see my moves during a fast song."

He bobbled his eyebrows and grinned devilishly. Jade laughed again. She could grow to like him a lot in a very short time.

Unable to resist the temptation, she moved her hand on his shoulder until she could touch his hair. It felt as soft as it looked. She curled her finger around a thick tendril.

His arm tightened around her waist. "Now you're making *me* crazy, just like when you drank from my glass."

Jade hoped the dim lighting would keep him from seeing her blush. "Your glass?"

"Don't pull that innocent act on me. You knew exactly what you were doing when you drank from the same spot I did."

She didn't think he'd notice that. It had been daring on her part, something she wouldn't normally do. But she'd wanted that intimacy, that moment of being one with him.

"I don't come on to my dates, Jade, no matter what you might think. I've never pushed a woman for sex."

"With your looks and charm, you wouldn't *have* to push."

"I appreciate the compliment, but I'm not looking for compliments. I'm being honest with you. I want very much to make love to you. But it has to be your decision. If you choose to say goodnight to me at your front door, I'll accept that."

The band flowed from the Bee Gees' song into "Always". Zach pulled her closer to him, so close she could feel how much he wanted her. Jade had to bite her lower lip to keep from moaning aloud. It'd been much too long since she'd had a man's hard cock inside her…

He nuzzled her neck, her earlobe. "You smell incredible," he rasped in her ear.

She'd turn into one big puddle of mush if he kept whispering to her. Jade tried to pull back, to put some distance between them. Zach didn't budge.

"Let me hold you like this. No pressure, I promise. Just let me hold you while we dance."

"May I cut in?"

Jade turned her head to see Doug Lassiter smiling at her. He wanted to dance with her? They'd been to many functions together, but he'd never asked her to dance. The man barely acknowledged her existence.

Zach released her and stepped back. He didn't look happy to hand her over to another man. "Certainly. I'll get us something to drink. Wine or tea, Jade?"

"Tea will be fine."

She watched him wind his way through the crowd until Doug stepped in front of her, blocking her view. Summoning a smile, she stepped into his arms.

*****

I'm gonna shove his nose up his ass if that bastard doesn't get it out of Jade's cleavage.

Zach silently fumed as he watched Doug Lassiter dance with Jade. Dance, hell. The man was trying to dry-fuck her right there on the dance floor. He admired the way Jade kept tugging away from him, despite Lassiter's attempts to keep her close.

The same thing had happened the first time she'd danced with the head of surgery. Zach had taken Jade back in his arms, only to be interrupted again by Dr. Jennings. After that, it'd been a man Zach hadn't met, followed by some guy who worked in the lab. Now Lassiter led Jade around the dance floor again, although it looked like he'd rather lead her to a bed.

Zach had only danced one song with Jade. That did *not* make him happy.

As soon as the song ended, she pulled completely away from the doctor. He saw Lassiter's mouth move, then Jade shake her head firmly before turning away from him. Her mouth thinned and her eyes narrowed in anger. Her strides carried her quickly toward Zach.

He met her halfway. "Are you all right?"

"I'm fine. I don't… I can't believe…" She huffed out a breath. "He's *never* done anything like that to me! He's the head of surgery and we're in *public*!"

"He's never come on to you?"

"No! Neither has anyone else at the hospital. What is *wrong* with the men tonight?"

Zach couldn't help chuckling at her confusion. She honestly had no idea why the men were drooling at her feet. Or rather, at her cleavage. "Men have been staring at you all night, Jade."

She blinked. "They have?"

"Look at yourself. You're hot. You look like you were poured into that dress."

Jade placed one hand over her breasts. "The dress is too much, isn't it? I told Breanna I should've worn something else."

"No, the dress isn't too much. You look beautiful in it."

Biting her lower lip, she rubbed her forehead. "I could get into such trouble. I *never* should've listened to my daughter."

Zach frowned, not understanding why she was so upset. "Why would you get in trouble? You have an incredible body. There's no crime in dressing to show it off."

"Zach, you don't understand. I represent the hospital. I have to be professional. Wearing a dress that shows so much of my breasts is *not* professional. The board could fire me over this."

"Over a *dress*? That's crazy."

"You don't understand how the board thinks. They expect their officers and representatives to be above reproach."

"You've done nothing that should cause your board any embarrassment. If anyone should be reprimanded, it's Doug Lassiter for humping you on the dance floor."

She clasped her hand over her mouth, but not before Zach heard her snort of laughter. He grinned. "Want me to rough him up a bit?"

"I wouldn't want you to hurt your hands."

"He looks pretty soft. One punch would be enough."

Jade laughed out loud. Zach pushed a curl behind her ear, then lightly caressed her jaw with his thumb. "Would you like to dance with me now?"

He saw a young man approaching them over Jade's shoulder. Zach tensed. Damn it, Jade was *his* date. He'd barely had two minutes with her in his arms. He could've said no when all those men cut in, but courtesy wouldn't let him. Besides, he didn't want to be rude to Jade's coworkers.

"I'd rather go home."

Her comment stunned him. Surely their evening wouldn't end yet. He wanted more time with her, more of a chance to get to know her better. "So soon?"

"Actually, it's not that soon. It's after eleven."

"Hi, Jade," the young man said once he'd reached them.

Jade turned and smiled. "Hi, Danny."

The kid tugged at his collar. His gaze darted to Zach before he looked at Jade again. "Would-would you like to dance?" he asked in a nervous, high-pitched voice.

"I'd love to, but Zach and I are leaving. Another time?"

His face fell with disappointment. "Oh, sure. No problem. Another time."

Jade touched his arm. "Thank you for asking, Danny."

Danny looked at her hand on his arm. Zach could actually see the kid's skinny chest puff out at that simple touch. He had to be eighteen, nineteen at the most, and obviously suffering from a huge crush on Jade.

Zach watched the kid shuffle away before he offered his arm to Jade. "Shall we go?"

Jade took his arm. "We shall."

Zach led her toward the exit, stopping only long enough to gather up her purse and wrap. She remained silent on the walk to the garage, and after they'd slipped into the car. He glanced at her before backing out of the parking space. She sat still in her seat, looking out the passenger window.

Zach waited until he'd pulled out of the garage before speaking. "You're quiet."

"I'm sorry. I was just thinking."

"About?"

She turned her head toward him. "About all those men who asked me to dance. I've never been the belle of the ball. Maybe I should wear low-cut gowns more often."

He could hear the humor in her voice. Zach grinned. "Well, I'll vote for that."

"Breanna talked me into buying this dress. I usually wear gowns that are more…well, I call them sedate. Breanna calls them boring."

"I think I like your daughter."

"There aren't many people who *don't* like Breanna."

"Like mother, like daughter. I'll bet you were very popular in school."

"I had a lot of friends."

"And boyfriends?"

"A few. But I lost all interest in any other boys when I started dating Carl."

"Is that your ex-husband?"

"Yes."

When she didn't continue, Zach prompted, "Do you still have feelings for him?"

"I'll always care about Carl because he's Breanna's father. He was the only man in my life for twenty years. But I don't love him. That died when he walked out on me." She groaned softly. "I can't believe I told you that."

Zach reached over and laid his hand over hers. "You can tell me anything, Jade. I'll listen, and I promise I won't judge."

Perhaps he should have moved his hand, but he didn't want to. He left it covering hers, his thumb making small circles on her fingers.

"Surely we can find other things to talk about than my ex-husband."

"Agreed. So, do you think the Cowboys will make it to the Super Bowl next year?"

Jade burst out laughing. Zach smiled at the light, feminine sound. He loved to hear a woman laugh.

He'd love to hear Jade moan in ecstasy even more.

She shifted in her seat and faced him. "Are you a football fan?" she asked.

"Guilty as charged. My brother and I watch the games together."

"Your brother?"

"Brent. I also have a sister, Michelle. I'm the oldest."

"I have one brother, Paul."

"The one on the fishing trip?"

"Yes."

Zach glanced at her. "Are you sorry your brother was out of town so your daughter had to hire me?"

"No," she said softly. "I've had a wonderful time tonight."

He squeezed her hand. "So have I."

All too soon, Zach pulled into the circular drive in front of Jade's house. He waited for her to say something, to invite him inside, but she remained silent, simply looking at him.

Their evening ended now. He'd walk her to her door, give her a soft kiss on the cheek, and leave. A heaviness formed inside his stomach at that thought. He could ask her out again…not as an escort, but as a man interested in a woman. Perhaps she'd say no, but he could at least try.

Zach climbed out of the car, rounded the hood, and opened Jade's door for her. Taking her hand, he helped her from the car, then slowly walked with her to the front door. He didn't want the evening to end, yet he had no choice. If Jade didn't invite him in, if she didn't want him, he'd leave with no complaint.

No outward complaint, anyway. Inside, he'd be crushed.

A sensor light came on when they reached her porch. Zach waited while she unlocked her door and dropped the keys back in her purse. She looked at him and smiled.

"Thank you for tonight. I had a good time."

"You're very welcome. It was my pleasure."

She shifted her small clutch from one hand to the other. Zach remained silent, sensing she wanted to say something else.

"Forgive me if I don't say this right, but am I supposed to tip you?"

It wasn't a stupid question. Women often tipped him, and quite generously, after an evening of sex. He didn't want money from Jade. He wanted time with her—something much more valuable than money.

"No, you aren't supposed to tip me."

"Oh."

She continued to look at him, but said nothing else. *Invite me in, Jade. I don't want our evening to end.*

"Good night," she said softly.

His heart dropped down to his feet. Leaning forward, he gently kissed her cheek. "Good night."

Zach watched her step inside her house and close the door. He remained on her porch for several moments, disappointment curling inside him. After releasing a deep breath, he headed for his car.

Chapter Seven

Jade leaned her forehead against her front door and closed her eyes. It'd been so hard to say goodnight to Zach instead of inviting him into her home. He was so thoroughly charming and gracious. She'd had to tell herself over and over that it was his job to be charming and gracious.

Yet it hadn't seemed phony or practiced. The erection he'd pressed against her on the dance floor had certainly been real.

He's a paid escort. He can probably get hard by simple wishing it. You can't have sex with him.

Jade had been the sexual aggressor in her marriage. While Carl often initiated their lovemaking and never said no when she initiated it, it was Jade who wanted to try new things, new positions. She'd been the one who'd wanted to spice up their sex life with toys. The suggestion of playing around with a dildo had been a blow to Carl's ego, as if she thought he wasn't enough to satisfy her.

She'd bet Zach had used every kind of sex toy ever invented. Her pussy clenched at the thought of trying out some of the more daring toys with him.

You're a mature woman, a woman who's been alone for two years. What's wrong with having sex with Zach this one time? What's wrong with using him for your pleasure?

Nothing, that's what.

Jade opened her door and scanned the driveway. Zach had started his car, but hadn't backed out yet. "Zach!"

He lowered his window. "Are you okay?"

"Yes. I was just wondering..." She swallowed to build up her courage. "We didn't get the chance to dance together very much."

"No, we didn't."

"Would you like to come in and dance with me now?"

He didn't answer her with words. Instead, he raised his window and turned off the motor.

The woman who had invited Zach inside to dance with her was a total stranger to Jade. She'd never been so forward with a man. She'd never had the *chance* to be so forward since she'd been married over half her life. Although she'd dated several men in the two years since her divorce, none of them had made her heart pound or her palms sweat.

Zach did that to her, and so much more.

She had a spacious living room, yet it seemed smaller with Zach standing in it. He was just so...*male*. Good looking, yes. Sexy, definitely. Also considerate, kind, and a wonderful dancer.

She refused to believe all the sweet things he'd said to her tonight were practiced lines of seduction. He hadn't been a rent-a-stud when he'd held her in his arms on the dance floor—he'd been a man who desired a woman. And she desired him just as fiercely.

So what if he happened to be ten years her junior? She wasn't going to marry him. She only wanted to touch him, have him touch her. Jade hadn't experienced that closeness with a man for two years.

She wanted that closeness with Zach...tonight.

"Do you have a preference?" Jade asked as she studied her rack of CDs. "Music or vocals?"

"Whatever you like will be fine."

She picked a CD of soft instrumental music that she particularly enjoyed. After placing it in the CD player, she faced Zach again. He stood with his arms at his sides, studying her intently. God, she loved his eyes. Such a striking blue, made even more blue by his tan skin. The tan probably covered a lot of him since he worked in construction.

The thought of finding out exactly how much of his body was covered by that tan made moisture dampen her thong.

Zach held out one hand to her. "May I have this dance, Ms. Talmage?"

With a tiny curtsy, Jade accepted his hand and moved into his arms. It amazed her how well they fit together. He held her close to him, yet loose enough so she could easily pull away if she desired.

She didn't want to leave his arms all night.

"I still think you were lying to me," Zach said softly.

Jade turned her head so she could see his face. "About what?"

"Stepping on my feet. You haven't stumbled once with me."

Say it, Jade. This is a one-time thing. Be completely honest with him. "Maybe I never had the right partner."

She rested her head on his shoulder. His hand swept up and down her spine in a slow, lazy caress. Jade sighed softly, content to follow his lead around her living room. To be touched, to be held, had never felt so good.

When the song ended and he tipped up her chin, she was more than ready for his kiss.

Velvety lips, his warm breath on her cheek, the barest flick of his tongue on her bottom lip. Jade experienced it all, and craved more. She whimpered when he cradled her cheek in his hand, tilted his head, and deepened the kiss. Clutching the back of his jacket, she parted her lips and accepted the gentle thrust of his tongue. Zach's free hand drifted down to her hip. He pulled her tighter against his groin. His cock felt hard and thick against her softness.

She wanted him inside her more than she wanted to see tomorrow.

A lingering caress of his thumb over her bottom lip stole Jade's breath. The corners of his mouth rose in a small smile.

"Very nice."

"Very," she whispered.

He drew her back into his arms and continued to dance when the next song began. He had to know she wanted him from her reaction to his kiss, yet he didn't hurry to get her naked. Instead, he held her, caressed her back, while leading her in the slow dance.

Jade didn't think it fair to compare men, but Zach was so very different from Carl. Carl had wanted sex, not lovemaking, when they started dating. He'd become more patient the longer they were together, but he'd never turned down an opportunity for sex. If he were here instead of Zach, she'd already be flat on her back with her legs spread.

What a wonderful difference. And an arousing one. Zach's consideration made Jade want him more.

Feeling bolder the longer they danced, she reached up and tugged on one end of his tie. Zach's steps faltered briefly, then continued. Slowly, she pulled the tie from around his neck and tossed it to the floor. Next came the onyx collar stud. She slipped it from the hole and parted his collar enough to press her lips against his throat. She smiled when she felt him swallow.

The next stud she removed gave her a tiny glimpse of his hair-dusted chest. She touched that spot with two fingertips. His skin felt damp.

"Are you hot?" she asked, looking up into his eyes.

"Yeah," he rasped.

"Why don't I take off your jacket?"

Zach released her and dropped his arms to his sides. Jade slid her hands up his chest to his shoulders, enjoying the firmness of his muscles on the journey. Gathering the jacket in her hands, she tugged it down his arms and let it fall to the floor behind him. She slid off his suspenders and let them hang at his hips. Slowly, oh so slowly, she began to release the rest of the studs on his shirt. A bit more of his skin came into view. Brown hair swirled over his chest and tapered down his flat stomach.

Jade couldn't stop a whimpering sigh. She loved hair on a man's chest.

Zach placed his hands back on her waist. Jade reached around him and unhooked his cummerbund. He dipped his head and pressed a kiss on her neck as she tugged his shirt from the waistband of his trousers. His lips moved up her neck, dropping kisses along the way. His tongue darted into her ear, then he suckled her earlobe.

Jade never knew her earlobe was an erogenous zone.

Her nipples beaded, her pussy wept. She wanted to draw out their lovemaking, make it last for a long time, but she didn't know if she could. She wanted him so much now, she didn't think it would be possible for her to wait much longer.

The shirt had to go. Longing to see his naked chest and arms, she pushed the shirt off his shoulders and down his arms, only to have it catch at his wrists.

Zach chuckled softly. "I think you forgot some of the studs."

"I think I did, too." She ran her fingertips down his chest to his waist and back up again. What a magnificent body. "Although I think I like you helpless like this."

His mouth quirked. "I never would have believed you'd be into bondage."

"I'm not. Or at least…" She slid one hand past his waistband. "…I wasn't until now."

He hitched in a breath when she touched his cock. Jade traced his shaft with her fingers, learning his shape and impressive size through the layers of cloth covering it. Her gaze shifted back and forth between his eyes and her hand. "There's something very…exciting about having control over you."

His breathing became deeper, heavier, as she caressed him. When she slipped one hand beneath his balls and squeezed, his eyes blazed.

"Get this damn shirt off me, Jade," he growled, "before I tear it off."

She smirked. His little temptress actually smirked. She was enjoying her power over him way too much. "I mean it, Jade."

"It's a beautiful shirt. Surely you don't really want to tear it."

Zach didn't give a damn about his shirt. He had a half-dozen shirts at home in his closet just like this one. The only clothing he cared about covered Jade's body. He'd tried to be patient. He'd danced with her, kissed her tenderly, held her close to him, when he wanted her naked and writhing beneath him. Patience could only go so far.

He'd reached his limit when she'd squeezed his balls. He wanted her clothes off *now*. "Unfasten the studs, Jade."

She did, although she took her time doing it. She'd barely had time to let the studs fall from her hand when Zach jerked off his shirt. He slipped one arm around her back, one under her knees, and lifted her.

"Where's your bedroom?"

"The end of the hall," she said, her voice breathless.

His strides ate up the distance in only seconds. Luckily, she'd left her bedroom door ajar, so he didn't have to release Jade to open it. He didn't want to let go of her until she lay on her bed.

Placing one knee on the bed, he lowered her to the thick comforter before reclining next to her. He cradled her face in one hand and kissed her thoroughly, the way he'd longed to kiss her ever since the first time he'd seen her. He used his lips, teeth, and tongue to make love to her mouth…sipping, stroking, nipping.

Her soft moan made his balls tighten.

He hated to leave that luscious mouth, but he had other places to explore. He led the way with his fingertips, followed closely by his lips. Her jaw received his attention, then the soft skin beneath her chin. He nibbled on her throat and soothed the small bites with his tongue. He dropped kisses on her collarbone, her chest, the top of one breast.

His last kiss earned him another moan.

Zach palmed her right breast as he slid his tongue into her cleavage. Locating her nipple with his thumb, he rubbed it until it became as hard as a pebble. He longed to have that nipple inside his mouth, beneath his tongue…

He longed to have his mouth on every part of her.

Zach continued to caress her breast while he rose up on one elbow. "I want to see you. Is the switch on the lamp or the wall?"

"The lamp," she whispered.

After one more deep kiss, Zach rose from the bed. He turned on the lamp, then faced Jade again. She looked beautiful lying on the earth-toned comforter. He didn't think his cock could get any harder. Watching her breasts rise and fall with her deep breathing, knowing she desired him as much as he desired her, made more blood surge into his shaft.

Zach unfastened his trousers and lowered the zipper. He was about to slide them over his hips when he noticed something out of the corner of his eye. A box sat on top of Jade's pillows, wrapped in green paper with a white bow. He frowned slightly. Who would've left a gift on Jade's bed?

"You have a present."

"What?" Jade turned her head when he gestured toward the box. Confusion filled her eyes. She sat up and reached for the box. "I don't understand."

Zach sat by her again and wrapped his arm around her waist. "Maybe there's a card."

After searching beneath the large white bow, Jade pulled out a small envelope. Zach looked over her shoulder as she withdrew the card and read it aloud.

"'To Mom and Zach. Have fun tonight. Bre.'"

Zach chuckled, both at Breanna's card and at Jade's blush. "Your daughter has quite a sense of humor."

"My daughter deserves to be spanked." She lifted the box onto her lap. "I'm afraid to open it."

"Would you like me to? It's addressed to both of us."

"I'm even more afraid for *you* to open it."

"Go ahead. It can't be that bad."

"You don't know my daughter."

Untying the bow, Jade raised the lid and pulled apart the bright green tissue paper. Several sex toys lay in the box. She gasped.

"Oh, my God. I can't believe she did this!"

She started to push the tissue paper back over the contents, but Zach held her hand to stop her. "Wait. Let's see what she bought."

"I am going to kill her, after I beat her."

Chuckling, Zach dug through the box, lifting the different items as he came to them. "Cock ring. Chocolate body paint. Stay-hard gel." He looked into Jade's eyes. "I don't think I'll need *that* tonight."

Her cheeks turned a deep pink. He dropped a kiss on her lips before beginning to explore again. "Anal beads. Ben-Wa balls. Fur-lined handcuffs. Nipple clamps. Lemon-flavored nipple cream." His gaze dipped to her breasts. "Interesting."

She huffed out a breath. "Can we close the box now?"

"Not yet. I like it when you blush."

Zach grinned when Jade scowled at him. "This is completely spoiling the mood."

"I won't have any problem getting hard again."

"Zach!"

Ignoring her outraged tone, he continued to sift through the items. "Lifelike dildo." He held it up to eye level. "Close, but not quite as big as I am."

Jade covered her eyes with one hand. "I don't believe this," she muttered.

"Butt plug. Wait, I'm wrong. It's a *vibrating* butt plug. *Very* interesting. I hope you have batteries. Never mind. Breanna included several packages."

"Okay, that's enough."

Jade tried to jerk the box out of his reach, but Zach held on to the side. "There're only a couple more items. We might as well see what they are."

"I don't *care* what they are."

"You might care about one of them." Zach held up a large box of condoms.

"Oh."

He turned the box in his hand. "I'm flattered, but I don't think I'll be able to use one hundred of these tonight."

"One hundred?"

"All different types, sizes, and colors."

Jade laughed. "Oh, Bre." She pushed her hair behind one ear. "What's the last thing?"

"Cherry-flavored lubricant. It looks like she thought of everything."

"You must think my daughter is crazy."

"I think your daughter loves you very much and wants you to be happy."

"That's true. But we won't use all this…stuff."

"Who says we won't?"

Chapter Eight

ꝏ

Zach's question left Jade speechless. She'd stood in her living room mere minutes ago and fantasized about using sex toys with Zach. While she fantasy was exciting, she couldn't be so bold with a man she barely knew. She had no problem with toys—loved them, in fact—but not with a man she hadn't known six hours ago.

"Do you have something against using toys, Jade?"

"No, of course not."

He touched her chest with one fingertip, drawing small circles on her skin. "Then what's the problem?"

"There isn't..." She stopped and swallowed. She couldn't possibly think straight with him touching her like that.

His finger dipped into her cleavage. "There isn't what?"

Zach continued his exploration with that lone finger, slipping it inside her bra and playing with a nipple. Jade's breathing grew uneven. "What?"

"You said 'there isn't'. There isn't what?"

She arched her back to bring her nipple closer to his stroking. "I don't know."

He leaned toward her. "Do you like me touching you?" he whispered in her ear.

"Yes."

He palmed her breast and gently squeezed it. "You're full and firm." His lips caressed her neck, her shoulder, as he squeezed her breast again. “I’ll bet your nipples are delicious.”

Jade whimpered.

Zach pulled his hand from her bra and stood. Looking in her eyes, he pushed his trousers and briefs over his hips.

He most certainly didn’t have any trouble getting hard again.

Jade rose to her knees and watched Zach slip out of his shoes, then his clothes. When it appeared he would climb back on the bed, she put up one hand to stop him. “Wait. Let me look at you.”

He stood still, arms at his sides. Jade absorbed the beauty of him…the wide shoulders, broad hair-dusted chest, flat stomach, lean hips, impressive cock, tight balls, strong thighs. She made the visual journey slowly, thoroughly enjoying every second of it. She’d seen pictures and videos of naked men, but Carl had been the only man she’d seen in real life. While he’d had a nice body, he couldn’t compare to the masculine perfection before her.

“Turn around,” she said, her voice raspy.

Zach did as she requested. She saw a scar beneath his right shoulder blade. Other than that one imperfection, his back was smooth. So were his buttocks. Nicely rounded, they would fill a woman’s hands as she gripped them while he pounded into her.

His tan covered his entire body. He either had help from a tanning bed, or he worked construction in the nude.

She’d bet the female neighbors would *love* that.

Jade moved closer to the edge of the bed. Reaching out one hand, she touched the small area of puckered skin. “How did you get the scar?”

“Fighting with my brother when I was ten. He pushed me to the ground and a stick gouged my back.”

She continued the gentle exploration of his skin with both hands. She caressed his shoulders, skated her fingers down his spine, cradled his buttocks. After thoroughly learning the back of him, she slid her arms around his waist. With her breasts pressed against him, she ran her hands up and down his chest and stomach.

"I'd like to touch you, too," he said over his shoulder.

"Not yet. I'm still enjoying you."

Jade began kissing his shoulders as she continued to caress him. She loved the feel of his hair-dusted skin against her palms. His nipples hardened as she passed her fingertips over them. Wondering if he received as much pleasure as she from having his nipples touched, she continued to caress them.

"Jade."

His voice sounded hoarse. Jade secretly smiled, loving the power she held over him. Taking his nipples between her thumbs and forefingers, she gently squeezed them. "Don't you like this?"

"I love your touch." He covered her hands with his. "But I want to touch you too."

"Soon."

She scooted closer and peered over his shoulder. His hard penis jutted forward, the head dark pink, the veins thick. Her mouth watered with the desire to taste him, to slide his shaft past her lips, her tongue.

Moving her hands farther down his body, she clasped his cock tightly. Zach drew in a sharp breath and released it when she cupped his balls.

"*God*, Jade."

She fondled his shaft, his balls, his upper thighs, then repeated the journey. Touching a man had never given her so much pleasure. She closed her eyes and continued to caress him blindly. Hardness beneath velvety skin. Tight testicles drawn up close to his body. Coarse hair at the base of his cock. A pearl of moisture on the tip. Jade savored all of it.

"Turn around," she ordered softly.

He faced her. Jade reached into Breanna's box and removed the bottle of lubricant. She flipped open the top and poured a generous amount into her palm. Looking into his eyes, she rubbed her palms together to distribute the cherry-flavored oil.

Zach closed his eyes and tilted his head back when Jade touched him. Her slick hands ran over every bit of his aching flesh. She didn't simply caress him—her hands made love to him. Opening his eyes again, he watched her fingers glide up and down his cock. She rubbed her thumbs over the sensitive head, teased his balls with only her fingertips.

A lot of women had given him hand jobs. None of them had brought him so close to his peak so quickly.

"Unless you want cum splattered all over that beautiful gown, I suggest you stop soon."

The impish grin she gave him made Zach want to grab her and kiss her senseless. "I guess that means you like this."

"Whatever makes you think that? The fact that I'm hard as a two-by-four?"

Her grin widened. "Well, since I don't want to explain cum spots on my gown to my dry cleaner, I suppose I should do something else."

She leaned forward and took the head of his cock in her mouth.

Zach sucked in a strangled breath. "Ah, Jade." Tunneling his fingers into her hair, he held her head and slowly began to pump his hips. This wasn't what he'd planned. He was supposed to love *her*, take care of *her*. That was his job.

Nothing with Jade felt like a job. This felt…right.

Her mouth slid down his cock and back to the head. The next pass of her lips took her farther down his shaft. Inch by inch, she gradually eased lower until she took all of him down her throat.

Few women had been able to take all of his penis without gagging. Jade knew how to give a blowjob, and obviously enjoyed it.

It'd be rude of him to ruin her fun.

Holding her head, Zach lazily pumped his hips in rhythm with her stroking hands and tongue. He'd trained himself to last, to hold off his climax as long as possible in order to give his partner pleasure. Holding off wouldn't be possible now. Her hands felt too good, her mouth too warm, for him to last long.

"I'm close, Jade." He wanted to warn her in case she didn't want him to come in her mouth.

Instead of backing off, she tightened her hand around his base. Knowing she wanted to taste him so intimately sent him over the top. With an animalistic groan, Zach filled her mouth with his seed.

It took him several moments to be able to think again. Once he became aware of his surroundings, he realized Jade still gently licked his softening cock. Cradling her jaws in his hands, he tipped up her face and kissed her. She tasted of cherries and him.

"Thank you," he whispered.

She smiled. "My pleasure."

"I could tell." He caressed her cheeks with his thumbs. "Would you like a drink?"

She shook her head. "I'm fine."

"It's my turn to give you pleasure now. All right?" He kissed her once more. "How about if I start by taking off your clothes? Swing your feet over here."

Jade shifted until she sat on the bed with her feet off the edge. Dropping to one knee, Zach removed the gold high-heeled sandal from her left foot. He took her foot in his hands and gently massaged it.

"Oh, that's nice," Jade sighed.

"A foot massage feels really good, doesn't it?"

"Heavenly."

After paying attention to her left foot for several moments, Zach removed the sandal from Jade's right foot and continued the massage. His fingers made the nylon slide over her skin, creating a *whoosh-whoosh* sound. "I give a great full-body massage. Are you interested?"

"Maybe after you…" She stopped and bit her lower lip.

Guessing what she'd been about to say, Zach continued. "After I make love to you?"

"Yes."

He squeezed her foot, then lifted it to his mouth and nipped her big toe. He would swear Jade's eyes crossed.

"Stand up for me."

Jade scooted off the bed and stood beside him. Still on one knee, he slipped his hands beneath the hem of her gown. He raised it slowly, exposing her body a few inches at a time.

His cock sprang back to full attention when he saw the lacy tops of her thigh-high stockings. His breathing quickened at the sight of the tiny scrap of emerald silk covering her pussy. It wouldn't take much more than a flick of his wrist to snap the elastic over her hips. The silk would fall away, leaving her open for his tongue.

He leaned forward and dropped a kiss on the emerald triangle. The scent of her arousal tickled his nose and made his cock throb.

Standing, he continued to raise the gown until it reached her breasts. "Lift your arms."

She did, and he pulled the gown over her head. His gaze dipped to her breasts as he dropped the gown to the floor. The skimpy emerald bra she wore barely covered her nipples. Her ivory flesh swelled over the cups as if asking to be kneaded, caressed, suckled.

Zach planned to do that…and a lot more.

"Get on the bed on your knees."

She gave him a puzzled look, but did as he asked. Moving to the center of the bed, she faced him with her arms at her sides.

"Spread your legs."

Heat flared in her eyes. Good. That's exactly what Zach wanted. He wanted her so hot, one pass of his thumb across her clit would make her come.

Zach waited until she'd obeyed his latest command before walking around the bed. She turned her head and watched him, yet didn't move from her position. He stopped behind her, inhaling sharply when he saw the thong between her round buttocks.

She had an incredible ass.

"I want you naked, Jade, but you look so sexy in your underwear and stockings. I am really enjoying the view."

He thought he heard her whimper.

"Arch your back."

The new position pushed her ass out farther. Zach couldn't resist touching her any longer. Placing one knee on the bed, he leaned forward and smoothed his hand over her buttocks. Nice and firm, as he'd suspected. He slid one finger up and down the cleft several times before circling her anus through the thong.

This time, he knew he heard her whimper.

Zach climbed up on the bed behind her. He continued to caress her buttocks while he slid his arm around her waist. His hand coasted across her stomach, over her breasts, between her thighs. Her thong felt warm and damp.

A woman's arousal had never been more important to him. He wanted to please Jade more than he'd ever wanted to please a woman.

He nipped the pounding pulse in her neck. "Spread your legs more."

Once she was open to him, Zach ran his left hand inside the front of her thong. Warm, thick cream covered her labia. "Mmm, you're really wet and swollen. I like that." He pushed his middle finger inside her. "And tight."

She sucked in a sharp breath. "It's been…awhile for me."

"Then I'd better loosen you up a bit." His index finger joined the first one. Jade moaned. "Am I hurting you?"

"No. It feels…Oh!…wonderful." She shifted her hips, moving them in a small circle. "More, please."

Granting her request, Zach pulled aside the elastic of her thong and slipped his right hand between her buttocks. He moved his left hand up to her clit. Picking up the cream from her pussy, he transferred some to her anus. He pushed two fingers back inside her pussy and his thumb in her ass as he rubbed her clit.

Jade hung her head and closed her eyes. "Too much?" Zach whispered in her ear.

"No. It's…" She gasped when he gently pinched her clit. "I'm almost… It won't take much more to make me come."

"Good. That's what I want. Concentrate on what I'm doing to you, how good it feels. Take your pleasure, Jade."

Her moan signaled the start of her climax. The contractions grabbed his fingers and thumb. Zach pushed both farther into her body and bit her neck. She threw her head back to his shoulder and bucked her hips as she rode out the wave.

Her labia still felt swollen to him. Suspecting desire still coursed through her body despite her orgasm, Zach continued to gently caress her. "Come again for me, Jade."

"I can't, not so soon."

"Yes, you can. Your body wants to. Let go and enjoy the feeling."

He began to pump his thumb in and out of her ass while continuing the attention to her clit. It took only moments for Jade to tremble from a second orgasm.

Zach nibbled her earlobe. "Told you so."

A bubble of laughter broke loose from Jade. "Stop sounding so smug." She pushed her hair back from her forehead. "My legs are weak."

"Do you want me to stop?"

"Oh, no!"

"Thank God."

She turned her head and looked at him. "It shouldn't feel so good. I've come twice, but your touch still feels so good."

"To me, too. But I think it's time to get you naked. Unsnap your bra."

Zach shifted to Jade's side so she could reach behind her. She removed her bra and tossed it off the bed. He gazed at large, creamy breasts with coral nipples. "Damn." Raising his left hand, he drew a circle around one areola. "Your breasts are beautiful. I have to find out if they're as delicious as they look."

Cupping the warm globe in his hand, Zach lowered his head and drew her nipple into his mouth. Her juices covered his hand. He could smell her unique scent as he suckled hungrily. Smelling wasn't enough; he needed to taste her, too. He alternated between sucking her nipple and licking her cream from his fingers.

Delicious.

Jade clasped his head and pushed her breast toward his mouth. "Oh, yes. Just like that."

Zach shifted his hand to her other breast, kneading it while he continued to suck her nipple. His right hand stayed busy between her thighs, caressing her feminine lips and anus. He knew he could make her come again with his fingers, but he needed more than that. He needed to have his cock buried to the balls inside her the next time she came.

Pulling his hands away from Jade, Zach kissed her before whispering, "Lie down."

She shook her head. "I think *you* should lie down."

Zach raised his eyebrows at her command. His little temptress had returned. Never one to disappoint a lady, he reclined on his back and folded his hands behind his head.

Jade climbed off the bed and slipped out of her thong and stockings. She returned to the bed, this time straddling his hips. Slowly, she lowered her body until her labia cushioned his shaft. Zach hissed in a breath.

"God, your pussy is hot."

"And your cock is hard."

Zach grinned. "I love it when you talk dirty."

"How about if I do more than 'talk'?"

"I'm game."

"Are you?"

Unsure what she meant by that question, Zach frowned slightly. His frown quickly faded when Jade reached into the box of "goodies" and withdrew the butt plug. "Do you plan to use that?"

She ran the fingers of one hand up and down the piece of soft pink plastic. "Mmm-hmm."

"Are you going to put it in, or are you going to let me do it?"

"I'm going to do it."

Zach swallowed hard, the mental picture of her inserting the plug into her body making his cock jerk. "I hope you realize I plan to fuck you while that plug is in your ass."

"Oh, I'm not going to use it on *me*." A wicked smile touched her lips. "I'm going to use it on *you*."

Chapter Nine

ℌ

If Jade hadn't been so turned on, Zach's startled expression would've made her laugh. She'd definitely surprised him.

She'd surprised *herself* by saying she planned to use the butt plug on him. The idea had simply popped into her head…the idea to do something daring with Zach, something she'd never done with Carl.

Throwing out the word "cock" a moment ago had also been daring for her. Jade had never used rough language of any kind.

It felt right to be open and honest with Zach in every way…and that included whatever words she wanted to use with him.

"Uh, what did you say?" Zach asked after clearing his throat.

"I have no doubt you heard me."

He pulled his hands from behind his head and laid them on her thighs. "I really don't think that's a good idea."

"Why not? Hasn't a woman ever used a butt plug on you?"

He snorted with laughter. "No."

"With all the women you've been with? I find that hard to believe." She rocked her hips, smiling to herself when he hissed. "Speaking of hard, you definitely are. The idea must appeal to you, at least a little."

"I have a beautiful, sexy, naked woman sitting on my cock. Yeah, it's gonna be hard."

Jade ran her fingers slowly up and down the plug. "That's the only reason you're so hard? It couldn't be because you find the idea…exciting?"

He didn't answer her questions. To Jade, that meant yes.

Reaching into Breanna's box again, she withdrew a package of AA batteries. She shifted her gaze back and forth from the toy to Zach's face as she inserted the batteries. His eyes heated, his breathing grew deeper, while he watched her.

Jade turned the small dial on the plug. "Oooh," she said when she felt the slight vibration. "Feel." She laid the plug close to his navel. Zach jerked and sucked in his stomach. Jade grinned. "This is going to be fun."

"You do realize I could flip you to your back in half a second, don't you?"

"Yes, but you won't." She leaned forward until her breasts brushed his chest. "You want to pleasure me."

"What I want to do is fuck you."

"I want that too, but not yet." She kissed him, her tongue dueling with his, before moving to his side. She turned off the plug and laid it on the bed. Locating the bottle of lubricant, she opened it and poured some on her fingertips. "Spread your legs, Zach."

Jade kissed him again as she touched his anus with her slick fingertips. She heard him groan deep in his throat. He grabbed her head, tilted it, and ravaged her mouth.

His fierce kiss made her legs weak all over again.

Jade returned his passionate kisses while rubbing the sensitive tissue. Thanks to the lubricant, her index finger slid easily inside him. He groaned again and lifted his hips.

"Does that feel good?" she whispered against his lips.

"Yes. God, *yes*."

She moved down his body as she continued the intimate caress. Each nipple received a nip with her teeth. She traced his navel with her tongue. She opened her mouth over the head of his cock and began a gentle suction.

"Jade, no. I don't want to come that way again."

"You won't." Holding tightly to the base, she held his shaft straight up and licked it like an ice-cream cone. "I won't let you."

She circled the head with her tongue several times before releasing him. This time when she picked up the butt plug, Zach's eyes flared.

After thoroughly lubricating the toy, she pressed it against his anus. He sucked in a breath through his teeth and closed his eyes. His hands clenched at his sides. "Am I hurting you?" she asked softly.

Eyes still shut, he shook his head.

Gently, Jade worked the toy inside him. The farther she pushed it, the heavier Zach breathed. She moved slowly, letting his body adjust to the sensation.

When she'd pushed the plug all the way inside him, she turned the control dial.

"Ah, *shit*!"

Zach arched his back. An almost pained expression crossed his face before he opened his eyes and looked at her. Jade had never seen such hot desire in a man's eyes.

"You have exactly ten seconds to get a condom out of that box and on my cock."

The time limit made her hands clumsy. Jade managed to open the box of condoms, then had no idea which one to pick. Frustrated, she turned the box upside down. One hundred condoms tumbled to her bedspread. "I don't know which one will…fit you."

Zach fumbled through the foil packets, finally choosing one that was bright blue. Quickly, he tore it open and slid the condom over his penis.

"Ride me, Jade."

He didn't have to tell her twice. Jade straddled his hips and lowered herself onto his shaft.

She gasped at the initial fullness. It'd been two years since she'd made love. Although she had a dildo and enjoyed using it, it couldn't compare to the real thing. Zach's cock felt so warm, so hard, so very *right* inside her. She tightened her internal muscles, earning another groan from Zach.

Unable to stay still any longer, Jade lifted her hips until he almost slipped out of her, then lowered herself again. Using Zach's firm chest for a brace, she began moving up and down, taking his cock deeper with each downward thrust.

"God, Jade, that feels good."

"It certainly does." She arched her back, trying to take him even farther inside her. "Mmm."

His gaze snapped to her chest. "I like it when you stick out your tits."

He gave her a lopsided grin that made her laugh. She couldn't remember ever laughing during sex. "You make me do things I've never done."

"Like what?" he asked before cradling her breasts in his hands.

"Like…" She drew in a breath when his thumbs skated over her nipples. "…laugh."

"Sex is fun. I want you to feel good. If laughing makes you feel good, I'll tell you jokes."

"No jokes. Just…this." She tightened her internal muscles again.

Zach exhaled sharply. "Oh, yeah. That works good."

Jade reached behind her thigh, located the plug control, and turned the dial higher.

"*Jesus*, Jade!"

"Do you want me to turn it off?"

"Hell, no!"

Jade couldn't help grinning. She liked doing something to him no other woman had done, especially when it gave him pleasure. "More?"

His eyes widened. "It'll go higher?"

"Mmm-hmm."

"I don't think I can take much more."

"Oh, I think you can." Jade turned the control dial to the fastest setting.

Zach's hips bucked, driving his shaft inside her far enough to make her catch her breath. The next instant, she gasped when he flipped her to her back.

"Enough playing," he said fiercely. "Now we fuck."

Zach hooked Jade's right leg over his arm, spreading her wider for his hard thrusts. His little temptress had crossed the line when she'd turned up the butt plug so the vibrations rattled his brain.

The fact that it felt incredible had nothing to do with it.

Opening his mouth over her neck, he alternated between licking and sucking her skin. He hadn't given a hickey to a woman in years, but he wanted to mark Jade as his. He wanted her to look in the mirror for several days and remember this night with him…the way he'd touched her, kissed her, fucked her.

Zach growled when she scratched his back. She apparently wanted to leave her own mark on him. Fine. He sucked harder on her neck as he pistoned his cock into her.

"Zach!"

Her breath hitched. Her back bowed. Her body shuddered. Zach continued the hard pounding while the orgasm grabbed her. Only after she stilled did he allow his own climax to peak.

Zach couldn't move. He lay still, his arm still hooked beneath Jade's leg. Both of them were covered with sweat. He knew she must be uncomfortable with his skin sticking to hers, but he wasn't sure if he could get any of his limbs to cooperate.

The insistent vibration in his ass made him move. He located the thin wire and followed it until he found the control dial. A flick of his thumb caused the vibration to stop.

"Wow," she breathed against his ear.

Zach chuckled. "Yeah."

"That was…intense."

Raising up on his elbows, he kissed Jade softly. "Intense is a good word to describe it."

"Was it just me? I mean, it's been two years since I've been with a man."

"No, it wasn't just you. It was intense for me, too."

He kissed her again, longer this time but still softly. He enjoyed it so much, he kissed her a third time before pulling away from her. "I'll be right back."

Zach stumbled into Jade's bathroom and shut the door behind him. He removed both the condom and plug, then located a washcloth so he could clean himself. As he stood at the sink, waiting for the water to run warm, he looked at himself in the mirror. He hadn't been exaggerating to Jade when he'd said their lovemaking had been intense. The closeness, the sensation of being one with a woman…it had never happened to him before tonight.

He wanted more.

Zach had no idea of the time, but it had to be after two. He'd never spent the night with a date. Coopers' Companions' rules didn't allow it, and he hadn't desired it either. Tonight, he'd break all the rules. He wanted to stay with Jade, to hold her for the rest of the night.

Rinsing out the washcloth, Zach laid it next to the sink and opened the door. Jade lay where he left her, in the middle of the bed, surrounded by sex toys. Part of him wanted to laugh at the sight. The other part wanted to devour that luscious body all over again.

She turned her head and smiled at him. "Hi."

He returned her smile as he walked to the bed. "Hi."

"I think there are one hundred condom packages stuck to my back."

"Only ninety-nine."

"True."

"Sit up and let me help you."

Zach knelt on the bed while Jade sat up. He chuckled when he saw several packages were indeed stuck to her back. "Well, there aren't ninety-nine here, but there are some." He plucked them from her skin and brushed the ones still on the bed away from her. "Better?"

"Much."

Her eyes were hooded, proof of her fatigue. Zach wouldn't mind a few hours of sleep either. "Ready for bed?"

"Definitely."

"Here." Climbing off the bed, he pulled back the covers so she could slide between the sheets. "I'll take care of the lights."

"Are you staying?"

"Yeah. Unless you don't want me to."

"I want you to very much," she said softly.

The luminous look in her eyes made Zach's cock stir. He could have her again. One kiss and he'd be hard. But she was obviously tired and needed sleep. For the rest of the night, he'd be content to hold her.

Zach made sure the front door was securely locked and all lights out before he returned to the bedroom. Jade lay on her side, facing the middle of the bed. She'd cleared all the sex toys off the bed, put them back in the box, and placed the box on her dresser. He'd expected her to shove the box under her bed or hide it in the closet. The fact that she hadn't told him she wouldn't mind playing with more of the toys.

His little temptress continued to delight him.

He turned off the lamp and slid into bed next to her. Cradling her face in his hand, he kissed her gently but thoroughly. "Turn over so I can hold you."

She did as he said, scooting her butt against his groin. Zach wrapped both arms around her and cupped her breasts. Dropping a soft kiss on her neck, he whispered, "Good night."

ChapterTen

ꙮ

Jade came awake slowly. She refused to open her eyes yet, hoping she could fall asleep again. She'd been having the most delicious, wicked dream about Zach and butt plugs…

The scent of roses tickled her nose. Frowning slightly, Jade moved her head on her pillow, searching for the perfect, comfortable spot again. She wanted to get back to that sexy dream.

A sensation of something moving over her chest forced her to open her eyes. She looked down to see a masculine hand dragging a white rose down her body.

Zach.

Jade turned her head to see Zach lying on his side next to her, propped up on one elbow. He grinned. "Good morning."

She smiled. Seeing Zach close to her was so much better than any dream. "Good morning."

The rose circled her left nipple, then her right. Jade arched her back as both nipples beaded. The covers had been pushed to the end of the bed, leaving her completely exposed to his gaze. Uncertainty sped through her, the fear he wouldn't find her as attractive in the light of day as he had in the soft lamplight.

A glance down his body at his very obvious erection quickly squashed her uncertainty.

The rose slid down her stomach and stopped at her navel. Jade quivered from the ticklish sensation. She reached for his hand to stop him…or she tried to reach for his hand.

That's when she realized her arms were above her head and completely immobile.

Jade twisted her neck so she could see her wrists. The fur-lined handcuffs kept her arms securely in place.

She whipped her head back so she could see Zach. A devilish grin turned up his lips.

"I had a hard time figuring out how to use those handcuffs since you don't have any slats in your headboard. So I had to improvise by tying a scarf around the post and attaching it to the cuffs." His grin widened. "Pretty smart, huh?"

Jade jerked her arms, but the cuffs and scarf stayed securely in place. "How did you do this without waking me?"

"I'm clever." He dragged the rose down the middle of her stomach to her pubic hair. "I wanted to try out some more of the toys. I figured the handcuffs were a good place to start."

His breath smelled of mint. Jade licked her lips, and winced at the awful taste in her mouth. He'd obviously been up and borrowed her mouthwash while her breath was bad enough to knock out an elephant. "Zach, let me get up for a minute."

He shook his head while moving the rose over her upper thigh. "Uh-uh. I have you right where I want you."

"I need to rinse my mouth. I promise I'll come right back."

Zach kissed her deeply. "You're delicious." He kissed her neck. "Very tasty." He flicked his tongue over one nipple. "Scrumptious, in fact."

He opened his mouth over the tip of her breast, sweeping the rose across her belly and hips as he suckled. The combination of sensations made her writhe on the bed.

She desperately wanted to touch him. "Zach, please take off the cuffs."

"Nope." Bending at the waist, he dipped his tongue into her navel before lifting his head and looking into her eyes. "It's my turn to do whatever I want to you."

"I won't stop you. I just want to touch you."

"No."

Jade huffed in frustration. She didn't fear he would hurt her. She had no doubt he only wanted to give her pleasure. But pleasure worked two ways. She wanted her hands on him, her fingers in his thick mane of hair.

His warm breath brushed across her labia. The tip of his tongue touched her clit. His position made his chin scrape over her thigh. The scratch of his morning stubble caused goose bumps to scatter across her skin. Jade sucked in her breath. "Zach, please."

"God, you smell good. I love the scent of an aroused woman." He laid the rose on the bed. Rising to his knees, he moved between her legs. He placed her feet flat on the bed, spread her thighs, and stared at her pussy. "You look good, too…all pink and swollen and wet." He gazed into her eyes. "Do you taste as good as you look?"

Feeling daring—and extremely aroused—she lifted her chin a bit. "Why don't you find out?"

He grinned. "With pleasure."

Zach lay between her legs and slipped his hands beneath her buttocks. Jade arched her back and bit her bottom lip to keep from crying out when he licked her slit. His tongue moved over her slowly, so slowly, as if he had all day to enjoy her. It circled her clit, slid over her labia, dipped into her ass. Over and over, he licked the feminine folds, making love to her with his mouth.

"Oh, *God*," Jade groaned, "you're really good at that."

He nibbled on the inside of her thigh a moment before returning to her clit. Jade moaned. Carl had been good at oral sex. Zach was incredible. He didn't rush, he didn't get rougher. He made love to her with his mouth as if he loved doing it.

Jade had always loved oral sex and always achieved orgasm. Never this fast or this powerful. The climax curled her toenails when it hit.

Zach had to realize she'd had an orgasm, yet he didn't stop. He continued to lick her slit, suckle her clit. Jade had barely come down from the heavens before she began the climb again. This time, she couldn't help crying out.

"*Zach*!" Lifting her hips from the bed, she pushed her pussy against his mouth. "Oh, *yes*!"

Jade struggled to catch her breath. When she managed to open her eyes, she saw Zach straddling her body on his hands and knees. His eyes practically glowed with heat.

"Taste how delicious you are," he growled.

He covered her mouth with his in a voracious kiss. Jade felt surrounded by her own scent and taste…and Zach. He cradled her cheeks while he kissed her again and again. His body held hers in place. With her arms handcuffed to the bed, she literally couldn't move.

She'd never felt so helpless…or so aroused.

He kissed each eye, her nose, her chin. "I'm gonna help you turn over on your stomach, all right?"

Right now, with the effect of two orgasms still flowing through her body, she'd agree to anything. She nodded.

Zach carefully helped Jade roll to her stomach. With the cuffs on her wrists, the new position made her arms cross. She now had even less room to move. Zach had never been into bondage or submission, but knowing she was almost helpless made his cock jerk.

Helpless or not, he had to make sure she was comfortable. "Are you okay?" he asked softly before dropping a kiss on her shoulder.

"Yes." She turned her head on the pillow and looked at him. "What are you going to do?"

"Play a little." He ran his hand down her spine and over her buttocks. "All right?"

She nodded her head.

"Can you raise up to your knees, or do you need me to help you?"

"I can do it."

Zach didn't think his cock could get any harder. Watching Jade struggle to her knees sent blood surging into his shaft. He slowly stroked it with one hand while she made herself comfortable on her elbows and knees. The new position raised her ass high in the air.

He had plans for that beautiful ass.

Crossing to the dresser, Zach located the lubricant and anal beads from the box of toys. He grabbed them and a condom and returned to the bed. Jade watched him the entire time. Her eyes widened when she saw what he held. Then they narrowed and turned sultry. She licked her lips and spread her legs another two inches.

Apparently, she wanted to play as much as he.

Zach climbed back on the bed between Jade's legs. He couldn't resist raking his teeth across each buttock. Jade's body jerked, making Zach grin. Oh, yes, this would be fun.

He sheathed his cock and glided it inside her. Jade groaned softly and lowered her head to her crossed arms. Flipping open the bottle of lubricant, he drizzled a thin stream of oil between her buttocks. Zach began slowly thrusting into her pussy as he spread the oil around her anus.

"You okay, babe?" he asked.

"Yeah."

"If I do something you don't like, tell me and I'll stop."

She didn't comment, but she also didn't pull away from him. Zach kept up the slow, easy thrusts while he lubricated the anal beads. He pushed one bead into her ass. She inhaled sharply. Zach waited for her to protest, but she remained silent. One by one, he added a bead until all eight were inside her.

Hot. Sexy. Desirable. Wanton. All those words to describe Jade flashed through his mind. He ran his hands up and down her spine and over her buttocks while he pumped into her. He loved the feel of her soft skin, the way she arched her back when he lightly scratched her buttocks. The sound of her breathing, the rapid rise and fall of her back, showed him she was close to having another orgasm.

Her contractions grabbed his cock. Zack took the string to the anal beads in his hand and tugged.

"Zach!"

One by one, he pulled the beads from her ass while she shuddered. Once the last bead popped free, he tossed the toy on the bed. Grasping her hips, he increased the speed of his thrusts until he pounded into her body. It wasn't enough; he had to get closer to her. He leaned over Jade's back and cradled her breasts in his hands. Squeezing her firm flesh, he continued to fuck her hard and fast. He heard her whimper and felt her walls begin to milk his cock again. A final hard thrust and he followed her over the edge.

The ability to think totally deserted him for several seconds. When his head stopped spinning, he realized Jade had to be uncomfortable. He reached up and released the lock on the handcuffs, then helped her straighten her legs. Still needing to be close to her, he reclined on top of her body, resting his weight on his elbows. His softening cock remained nestled inside her warmth.

He dropped soft kisses on her neck and shoulder. "You okay?" he whispered.

"Mmm."

Her answer made him chuckle. "How many times did you come?"

"I lost count."

"I know of at least three."

"At least." She pushed her hair off her forehead. "I won't be able to walk for a week."

"That's the wonderful thing about sex—you heal fast."

He smiled at the sound of her laughter. He enjoyed hearing her laugh, almost as much as hearing her moans of ecstasy.

Zach kissed her nape. "Would you like me to move?"

"Yes and no. I'm very comfortable, but I really need to use the bathroom."

"Definitely my cue to move." He dropped one more kiss on her nape before slowly withdrawing his cock from her pussy. "I'll start some coffee."

"I'll kiss your feet if you start coffee."

"I'm sure you can think of better places to kiss." Zach stood and helped her from the bed. "Speaking of kissing..." Both nipples received the loving caress of his tongue. "Those need a lot more kissing today, don't you think?"

Jade cleared her throat. "That works for me."

Cradling her cheek, he ran his thumb over her lower lip. He didn't want to leave her yet. "Do you mind if I stick around for a while?"

"I'd like that."

He jerked his head toward the bathroom. "Go do your thing and I'll start the coffee."

Jade found Zach reclining on her bed when she opened the bathroom door. He lay on his back, one arm over his eyes. For a moment, she stood still and feasted on him. Even relaxed, his shaft looked thick and long and oh so nummy. She knew for a fact how big it felt inside her. From his tan skin to his broad chest, from his flat stomach to his strong thighs, everything about Zach's body made her hormones scream.

His attentiveness, his consideration, made her heart swell. A woman could fall for him before she had the chance to stop it.

It's his job to be attentive and considerate, Jade. Don't forget that.

He moved his arm and looked at her. A gentle smile turned up the corners of his mouth. "Feel better?"

"Much."

"Coffee's on. It should be ready soon."

"It smells wonderful."

She walked to the bed and lay beside him. Zach rolled to his side. Propping up on his elbow, he rested his other hand on her stomach. "I have an idea."

"What?"

"Let's shower together, then I'll take you out to brunch. A friend of mine owns a restaurant in the Hulen area. He serves an incredible Sunday brunch until two. After that, we can go to a movie. Your choice." He grinned. "I'll even suffer through a chick flick if that's what you want to see."

"You want to shower with me?"

"Yeah. Is that a problem for you?"

"No. I just... I don't know..." Jade stopped and bit her bottom lip, unsure how to voice her questions.

Zach inched his hand higher until it rested beneath her left breast. "You don't know what?"

"Do you usually do this? I mean, Breanna paid for you to escort me to the gala. She didn't pay for anything else. Did she?"

A slight frown drew his eyebrows together. "No, she didn't pay for anything else." He cradled her breast in his palm. "I want to spend more time with you, Jade...you and me, a man and a woman. It has nothing to do with me being an escort. It has to do with me wanting to be with you, getting to know you better." His thumb whisked across a nipple. "I've never spent the night with a date, Jade." Leaning over, he dropped a soft kiss on her lips. "I wanted to stay with you last night, to hold you and wake up with you in my arms this morning." A crooked grin tipped up his lips. "The wild sex was a bonus."

Jade giggled.

"I'd like to spend the rest of the day with you...and the night, if you think you can put up with me that long."

She caressed the hand covering her breast. "I don't think that'll be a problem."

Chapter Eleven

ꕥ

Jade tilted her head back to rest on Zach's shoulder. The warm water from the shower flowed over her stomach and thighs while his hands ran over her breasts. He'd told her he only wanted to help her bathe. The amount of time he'd spent soaping her breasts had to mean they were cleaner than they'd ever been in her life.

She had no intention of stopping him.

Sighing, she reached behind her and clasped his neck. "Your hands feel so good."

"So do your breasts." He plucked at her hard nipples. "I love touching them."

"I've noticed."

He nuzzled her ear. "Are you complaining?"

His warm breath made her shiver. "No way."

Jade felt him smile against her neck. "Good, 'cause I don't plan on stopping. In fact…" One hand slid down her stomach to between her thighs. "I'd like to be inside here again."

It couldn't be possible. They'd made love less than twenty minutes ago. He couldn't get hard again so soon.

The press of his erect cock between her buttocks proved her wrong.

Zach pushed two fingers inside her pussy. Jade flinched and gasped softly. Muscles she hadn't used in two years protested his touch.

"Sore?" he asked.

"A little."

"So turning you around and fucking you against the wall is out?"

Jade laughed at his language. Carl had never spoken to her like that, not even in the heat of desire. She turned her head so she could see his face. Devilment danced in his eyes.

"May I have a rain check?"

He smiled and pulled his fingers from her body. "Absolutely."

So close to that luscious mouth, Jade couldn't resist tugging him closer so she could kiss him. One kiss led to two, then three, until she found herself plastered against the wall while Zach devoured her mouth.

"I love kissing you," he growled against her lips.

"And you are *so* good at it."

He grinned. "Like my technique, huh?"

"Very much. You've had a lot of practice to master that technique."

His grin faded. "Yeah, I've had a lot of practice. I've been with a lot of women. I won't apologize for that." He plowed his fingers into her wet hair. "Everything became mechanical to me. I performed like a robot—insert tab A into slot B. Maybe that's crude, but that's how sex seemed to me, at least part of the time. I do love sex. I love all the intense feelings, the closeness with a woman, the moment just before a climax when you focus on nothing else except what's happening in your body." He kissed her. "But it was a job, and it began to feel like a job. I don't like that. With you…" He stopped and tilted up her face for another kiss. "I told you I've never spent the night with a date. I swear that's true. But you aren't just a date to me, Jade. You make me feel…" He kissed her again. "You make me feel things I've never felt. I want to explore those feelings."

Jade swallowed hard. He painted a beautiful picture, but he was moving way too quickly. "We barely know each other, Zach."

"All the more reason to spend more time together, so we'll get to know each other better."

"You can't possibly be…interested in me."

He frowned. "Why do you say that?"

"I'm ten years older than you."

"What does that have to do with anything?"

Before she had the chance to answer his question, her stomach growled loudly. Jade blushed while Zach grinned.

"Hungry?" he asked.

"Starving."

"Let's get out of here and go to brunch." He kissed her once more. "We'll talk more about this later."

Zach watched Jade as she dried her body with a large dark green towel. He clutched his own towel in one hand, so absorbed with looking at her that he ignored drying himself. Last night, she'd been dressed to look her best at the gala with hair and makeup perfect. Now, she stood before him nude, fresh out of the shower, no makeup, with droplets of water still dotting her skin.

She was even lovelier now than last night.

His cock responded to the sight of her. Zach moved the towel to cover his groin so Jade wouldn't see his growing hard-on. She'd told him she was sore, and he respected that. He wouldn't push her to make love again until she was ready.

Even though he wished he could be inside her again right now.

His high sex drive could be considered a curse or a blessing. Zach loved sex and he loved it often. His dates never seemed to mind that he could get hard more than once in a short period of time. With practice, he'd learned to hold back his own orgasm to please his partner first. He could fuck as long as it took for her to come, whether that be two minutes or twenty.

He'd quickly become Coopers' Companions most requested escort because of his…special talents.

Standing here, looking at Jade, he couldn't imagine being intimate with any other woman but her.

Lowering his gaze, he began to dry his body. So many feelings were bouncing around inside him, feelings he'd never experienced. He wanted to take her to brunch so he could talk to her while they were relaxed, try to sort out everything.

He'd never been in love, so didn't know how it felt. He strongly suspected his blossoming feelings for Jade could quickly turn into love.

"Zachary Cooper!"

Her screech shocked him. Zach jumped and dropped his towel. He raised his head to see Jade staring into the mirror. "*What*?"

"You gave me a *hickey*!"

Her horrified expression made him laugh. She scowled at him in the mirror. "It isn't funny."

"It won't last, Jade."

"But it'll be there tomorrow when I go to work." She turned her head and stared at the mark. "It's the size of Grand Prairie!"

Zach walked up behind her and slipped his arms around her waist. Moving her hair aside, he dropped a kiss on the hickey. "You didn't complain last night when I gave it to you."

"Well, of course I didn't complain last night. I was...busy."

He grinned and tightened his arms around her. "I know."

When she continued to frown, Zach tried another tactic. "Your hair will cover it. And you can use makeup, can't you?"

"I suppose."

"Why are you so upset? Are you afraid someone might know you had..." He dropped his voice to barely a whisper. "S-E-X?"

Her frown faded and she bit her bottom lip. "Am I overreacting?"

"Yeah, I'd say that."

"I'm sorry. It's just... I'm a total professional at my job, Zach. I never mix personal with business."

"I don't doubt that."

She tilted her head and studied the large discoloration. "I suppose I should be proud of it. I haven't had a hickey in at least twenty years."

"Glad to be of service." The reflection of her breasts in the mirror was too tempting to ignore. He slid his hands up to cup the heavy globes. "I'd be happy to be of service again right now."

She laughed out loud. "Are you ever going to feed me?"

"Are you ever going to get dressed and stop distracting me with this incredible body?"

"I think you're perpetually horny."

"I am with you, that's for sure."

She grinned. "I like that."

Zach swatted one rounded buttock. "Get dressed, woman."

Still grinning, Jade clutched her cheek and skittered into the bedroom.

Jade had donned bra and panties when Zach came out of the bathroom. She watched him round the bed and pick up his tuxedo trousers from the floor.

"You're wearing a wrinkled tuxedo to brunch?"

"Hardly." Not bothering with his briefs, he slipped on the trousers. "I have a duffel bag in my trunk with a couple of changes of clothes in it."

"I guess that comes in handy the morning following a date."

Zach walked back to her. He placed one finger beneath her chin and tilted up her face for his kiss. "I told you I've never spent the night with a date. But sometimes I spend the night at my brother's place. He's slimmer than I am, so I keep clothes in my car."

"Oh." The heat of embarrassment filled her cheeks. She'd sounded almost…jealous. How silly. After today, she'd probably never see Zach again.

Amusement crinkled the corners of his eyes. He dropped one more soft kiss on her lips. "Be right back."

A hollow feeling formed in Jade's stomach that had nothing to do with the lack of food. She didn't like the idea of never seeing Zach again. She'd known him less than twenty-four hours, yet it seemed longer. She enjoyed talking to him. She liked his teasing, his crooked grin. The sex was mind-boggling, but it was more than sex with Zach. She hadn't "clicked" with a man since Carl. She'd dated several men, yet never had the desire to go out with them again, much less have sex with them. The interest simply hadn't been there.

He'd started out as a rent-a-stud, but that's not how she thought of him now.

Jade sank down on the bed. She couldn't do this. She couldn't develop feelings for a man ten years her junior. They couldn't possibly have a future together. Falling in love with Zach would only lead to heartache.

He came back in the bedroom carrying a dark blue bag. He stopped next to the bed. "You okay?"

The concern in his eyes made her scramble for something to say. "Just trying to decide what to wear."

"Ah, a girl thing." Zach dropped the duffel on the bed. "I vote for something that shows off your tits."

Jade laughed while he grinned. "You really are a sex fiend."

"Guilty as charged." Resting one knee next to her, he cradled her neck and kissed her. "You have a beautiful body, Jade. Be proud to show it off."

She didn't get the chance to respond to his compliment for the phone rang. After one more kiss from Zach, she picked up the receiver. "Hello?"

"It's almost noon," Breanna said with a hint of impatience in her voice. "Why haven't you called me?"

"It's Bre," she said softly to Zach.

"I'll get dressed in the bathroom to give you some privacy."

"Mom!"

"I'm here."

"Were you talking to someone?"

"Yes, I was talking to Zach."

"Ohmigod, he's still *there*? He spent the *night* with you?"

"He did."

"Wait, let me get comfortable. Okay, I'm ready. I want *all* the details."

"We're getting ready to go to brunch. I can't talk now."

"At least tell me he's hung and you had four or five orgasms."

"I can't believe the language that comes out of your mouth."

"You're changing the subject."

"I am. I have to finish getting dressed. We'll talk later."

"You can't leave me hanging, Mom! Zach told me he *never* spends the night with a date."

Breanna's comment left Jade speechless for a moment. "And just when did he tell you that?"

Silence. Jade could picture her daughter biting her lower lip, the way she did when she was stalling.

"Oops."

"'Oops' is right. What did you do, Bre?"

"Uh, I gotta go, Mom. Have a nice brunch."

"Breanna!"

Clunk.

Jade replaced the receiver and hurried into the bathroom. She found Zach sitting on the toilet lid, pulling on a pair of white socks. He looked up and smiled.

"That was a short conversation."

"But very enlightening." She crossed her arms over her stomach. "Did you talk to my daughter before we went to the gala?"

Zach slowly straightened. His smile faded. "Did she say that?"

"Do *not* answer a question with a question. Did you talk to my daughter?"

He released a breath. "Yeah, I did."

"When?"

"Yesterday. She left a message for me to call her, so I did."

"What did you talk about?"

He stood and stepped close to her. "She loves you, Jade. She only wanted to make sure you had a good time at the gala."

"Why don't I believe that's all she said?"

"We…discussed some other things."

"Like what?"

Zach ran his hand around the back of his neck. "Shouldn't you ask Breanna that?"

His obvious discomfort made Jade even more suspicious. "I'm asking *you* and I expect an answer."

Stepping closer, he ran his hands up and down her arms. "She said she wanted you to have a good time in every way…including sex."

Hearing him say the words, Jade still couldn't believe him. "What?" she asked weakly.

"She wanted to be sure we made love. I told her that would be *your* decision. I meant that, Jade. I've *never* pushed a date for sex."

"She actually talked to you about having sex with me?"

"Don't be angry at her, Jade. She loves you."

Tears of mortification filled her eyes. "You had sex with me out of pity?"

"No!" Zach tightened his hands on her arms. "Don't you ever say that. I wanted to make love to you. I still do. Pity has nothing to do with it. My God, don't you know how beautiful and sexy you are?"

"My daughter must not or she wouldn't have hired a man to have sex with me."

"Jade, she told me you hadn't been with a man since your divorce. She wanted you to feel desirable and appreciated as a woman." He wiped away a tear on her cheek with his thumb. "I told her I would never do anything to make you uncomfortable. She wanted me to initiate sex because she said you wouldn't. I told her no."

"You did?"

Zach nodded. "My main job as an escort is to be an escort. If my date doesn't want a more intimate ending to our evening, I accept that. I would've left you at your front door if that's what you'd wanted."

"I wanted *you*."

"I'm glad," he said softly before covering her lips with his.

Chapter Twelve

ဢ

Jade rested her head against the loveseat and thought about this afternoon. Brunch had been delicious. Jade smiled as she remembered the way he'd fed her bites of his French toast when she "hinted" that she wished she'd gotten some off the buffet. They'd shared each other's bodies, yet eating from his fork seemed so intimate…something only an involved couple would do.

His witty conversation and double-entendres had made the meal fun.

As promised, Zach took her to the movie of her choice after brunch. She could tell she'd surprised him when she'd opted for an adventure instead of a sappy romance. Not that she didn't love sappy romances, but she'd picked something she thought he would enjoy also.

They'd come back to her house, only to have him leave again immediately. When she'd questioned him, he'd told her he had a couple of errands to run and would be back soon.

That "soon" turned into an hour and a half. Since he'd come back, he'd been hiding out in her kitchen. She assumed he'd bought some kind of food items, but she didn't know for sure. He'd parked at the back of her house and used the rear entrance into the kitchen. Whatever he'd brought in remained a mystery to her.

He'd told her to stay put, but curiosity gnawed at her. Jade's living room led into her dining room, which led into the kitchen. She normally loved the layout of her house, but now wished her living room connected to the kitchen so she could see Zach. He'd been mysterious ever since they'd come home from the movie.

"What are you doing in there?" she called out so he could hear her.

"You'll find out in a minute. I'm almost through."

"Can I come in and get a glass of tea?"

"No."

"Hey, this is *my* house."

"Patience, Grasshopper. All will be revealed to you soon."

She couldn't help chuckling at his really bad Chinese accent. "You make a lousy David Carradine."

"My talents lie elsewhere."

"That's for sure," she said to herself, thinking of his talent as a lover. All his years as an escort had certainly been worth it. His kisses made her weak, his caresses made her blood pressure skyrocket. His tongue…

Jade sighed. Ah, his tongue. The rasp of it over her nipples, the playful dips into her navel, the long, slow licks up and down her labia. Zach certainly knew how to use his tongue to send her desire over the edge where it had never been.

It should be registered as a lethal weapon.

She'd been married for nineteen years and had never experienced the passion, the craving, that Zach made her feel.

Jade had been so hurt when Carl left her, she'd vowed never to trust another man. Two years alone had made her rethink her vow. While she enjoyed her independence, she didn't want to spend the rest of her life alone. She wanted to share her life with someone…someone considerate, funny, caring.

Someone like Zach.

It wouldn't be difficult at all to fall in love with him. He had all the qualities she wanted in a man, besides being an incredible lover. If he were her age, she wouldn't hesitate to become involved with him. Even two or three years younger would be fine, but not ten. She couldn't imagine getting over that much of a hurdle.

She knew she was getting ahead of herself. Thinking of Zach as anyone other than an escort would be silly. He'd said this morning he wanted to get to know her better. That didn't mean he wanted anything more than what they shared this weekend. He was a young, handsome, virile man who had no reason to become involved with an older woman. Besides his job that required his single status, there were dozens of young, attractive women who could offer him so much more than she.

A movement to her left made Jade turn her head that direction. Zach came out of her dining room carrying one of her large bed trays. She gasped softly. He'd changed into a pair of cut-off gray sweatpants. The fleece looked soft and worn, and conformed perfectly to every ridge of his penis. He obviously wore nothing else.

Jade swallowed.

"Are you hungry?" he asked with a smile.

Oh, boy, am I ever! I'd love to munch on you. Instead of saying what she thought, she cleared her throat and returned his smile. "What did you do?"

"I made us a snack."

He set the tray on the floor before sitting beside her. Jade glanced over the array of dishes. He'd cut everything into bite-size pieces. She saw shrimp, chicken, grapes, strawberries, orange slices, two kinds of cheese, brownies, and a bowl of creamy dip. "You call this a *snack*?"

"Okay, it's a big snack." He grinned. "I'm a growing boy."

Jade pointedly looked at his groin. "You won't be able to hide that fact in those shorts."

"I wanted to get comfy." He fingered the lapel of her chambray shirt. "Maybe you should get a little more comfy too."

Taking his advice, Jade slipped off the long-sleeved shirt. His gaze dropped to her breasts. The appreciation in his eyes made her glad she'd worn the formfitting white tank beneath her open shirt. "Better?"

He slipped one finger inside the waistband of her jeans. "How about taking these off too?"

Instead of answering his question with words, Jade released the snap and slowly lowered the zipper. Zach watched her as she lifted her hips from the floor and slid her jeans down her legs. She kicked them off to land in a puddle at her feet. "Better?" she asked again.

"Oh, yeah." Zach slowly ran one hand up the inside of her leg from knee to thigh. He curled his fingers beneath her upper thigh, a mere inch from her pussy, and kissed her shoulder. "Much better. And before I get totally distracted by your incredible body, I'd better get the wine."

Jade watched him rise and walk toward the kitchen. His cutoffs fit his butt as snugly as his penis.

A man that gorgeous should come with the warning label "Caution: Dangerous to hormones".

He'd told her she had an incredible body. She'd never thought of herself that way. To her eyes, she'd always been plump. Zach made her feel beautiful. Sexy.

Sensual.

Jade slipped her hands inside her tank top and unhooked her bra. She tugged the straps down her arms, pulled the bra from beneath the tank, and tossed it on the floor on top of her jeans where Zach would be sure to see it.

He returned with a bottle of Chardonnay and two wineglasses. He looked at her face as he walked toward her, then his gaze shifted to her pile of clothing. He stopped and studied the bra on top of the pile. A slow, sexy grin tipped up his mouth when he looked back at her, his attention on her unbound breasts.

"Got even more comfy, huh?"

"I didn't think you'd mind."

"Nope. Don't mind at all. I love looking at your nipples."

Zach returned to his position on the floor next to Jade. He silently told his randy cock to behave, that he wanted this time to be romantic for Jade. It didn't listen. Seeing that tiny strip of skin between the bottom of her tank and the top of her bikini panties made his penis immediately stand up and take notice.

The sight of her hard nipples through the soft cotton didn't help to calm anything down, either.

He poured her wine and handed her the glass. "To a romantic evening together."

"I'll drink to that," she said softly.

Zach poured his own wine and set the bottle aside. After touching his glass to hers, he sipped the cold liquid, watching as Jade sipped her own. God, she was lovely. Those huge green eyes, the ivory complexion, the incredible auburn hair, the full lips made for kissing…

Or sliding over his cock.

Clearing his throat, Zach picked up a toothpick and speared a piece of shrimp. He lifted it to Jade's mouth. "Open wide."

A devilish twinkle lit up her eyes. "I'd love to."

He playfully scowled at her. "Behave."

"Zach, you're sitting there with a huge hard-on. Surely you know I see it."

"I'm trying to be a gentleman here." He nudged her mouth with the shrimp. Jade parted her lips and accepted his offering. Her teeth clamped around the toothpick and slowly dragged the shrimp into her mouth, holding his gaze the entire time.

Zach's cock jerked.

"I think," Jade said, placing her glass on the bed tray, "I need to do something about your…problem."

"I want to concentrate on *you*, Jade."

"You can." She took his glass and set it next to hers. "But that doesn't mean I can't play with you at the same time."

Anticipation warmed his blood as Jade rose to her knees and moved toward him. Zach spread his legs, giving her room between them. She scooted forward until her knees lightly pressed against his balls. Tunneling her fingers into his hair, she tipped back his head. He watched her gaze travel over his face, almost as if she wanted to memorize every feature.

"You're a gorgeous man, Zachary Cooper," she said softly.

He cradled her buttocks in his hands and tugged her an inch closer. "You're a beautiful woman, Jade Talmage."

"You make me feel beautiful. You make me feel…"

She stopped. Zach waited for her to continue. When she didn't, he prompted, "I make you feel what?"

She sighed softly. "You just make me *feel*."

She kissed him, long and slow and deep. Zach ran his hands over her buttocks and back while her tongue made love to his mouth. He loved the way she kissed, as if she couldn't get enough of his mouth, his tongue. She reacted the same when he fucked her, as if she couldn't get enough of him thrusting his cock deep inside her.

She ended the kiss and rested her forehead against his. "Do you know it's been over seven hours since you made love to me?"

"I should be horsewhipped."

She smiled as she continued to run her fingers through his hair. "In all fairness, part of that is my fault."

"I did offer to fuck you in the shower and you said you were sore."

"True."

"So you aren't sore any more?"

She shook her head. "All better now."

Zach slipped his hands beneath her tank top and caressed her breasts. "Do you have something particular in mind?"

"Mmm-hmm, if you're willing."

He circled her nipples with his thumbs. "I believe you'll find I'm willing to do just about anything. Remember the butt plug?"

"I *do* remember. That was fun." Jade pulled off her tank and tossed it on top of the rest of her clothing. "I'm thinking of a number between one and one hundred."

Zach was so busy admiring the creamy globes he held in his hands, it took him a moment to realize what she'd said. He raised his gaze back to her face. "A number?" The light bulb went off in his head at the mischievous look in her eyes. "A *number*. Like maybe…sixty-nine?"

"The man wins the prize on the first guess."

He grinned. "That just happens to be my favorite number."

"Well, then." She slid her hands down his chest to the waistband of his cutoffs. "I think the first order of business is to get these off."

Zach lifted his hips so Jade could tug off his shorts. He expected her to remove her panties also. Instead, she bent over and took his cock in her mouth.

"Hey, no fair. I'm supposed to..." Zach hissed in a breath. "God, your mouth is warm."

She also sucked cock as if she couldn't get enough. Her tongue swirled around the head, dipped into the slit, slid up and down the thick veins. How easy it would be to let her bring him to a climax with her mouth, the way she did last night. He didn't want that. He wanted to be buried deep inside her tight pussy when he came.

That didn't mean he couldn't enjoy her mouth for a while.

Zach shifted so he could lie on the floor. She followed him, not releasing his shaft from that warm wetness. Once he'd gotten comfortable, he lay still and let her do whatever she wanted. She licked his shaft over and over, then moved to his balls. She licked them thoroughly, then moved back to his penis. One long, slow glide of her lips had him all the way down her throat.

When she pushed one finger in his ass, Zach knew he had to stop her. "Hey," he said softly.

She raised her eyes and looked at him, but kept licking his cock. "What?"

"My turn."

Her tongue circled the head twice before she spoke again. "You want to spoil my fun?"

"No, I want to return the favor."

She stood long enough to remove her panties before returning to her knees and taking him in her mouth again.

Zach enjoyed the sensation of warmth and wetness for a moment before he touched her head. "Swing around here, Jade. Let me lick that pretty pussy."

Without taking her mouth off him, Jade shifted her body until she straddled his face. Zach inhaled deeply of her musky, feminine scent before spreading her labia with his thumbs. Her lips were dark pink and swollen. Her creamy juices flowed freely. Her clit peeked out as if begging for attention.

He was only too happy to give it all the attention it wanted.

A long, slow lick of her slit had Jade moaning. God, she tasted good, like sex and desire. Another lick made her squirm. When he closed his lips around her clit and suckled, she released his cock and arched her back.

"Zach!"

He'd planned to take time with her, to lick her pussy slow and easy until he made her come. Sucking on his shaft had obviously turned her on so much, slow and easy wouldn't be enough. Zach held on tightly to her ass and devoured her, his tongue and lips moving quickly over her clit.

He pushed one thumb inside her ass, and she shattered.

Several seconds passed before she lowered her body on top of his. Zach assumed she'd take his cock in her mouth again and finish what she'd started, which would have been perfectly fine with him. His little temptress surprised him again. Instead of doing what he expected, she turned around, took his penis in her hand, and impaled herself.

Zach hissed. "Oh, *fuck*!"

"That's exactly what I intend to do."

Chapter Thirteen

ꟹ

He filled her completely. Jade closed her eyes and luxuriated in the feeling of Zach so deep inside her. She didn't move, but simply relished that fullness.

The subtle shifting of his hips made her look at him. She saw heat. His blue eyes almost gleamed with heat.

"Fuck me, babe," he whispered. "Take me however you want me."

His graphic language sent a zing through her clit, despite her recent climax. Jade didn't know her body was capable of such intense sensations. Sex with Carl had been good, but this went so far beyond good.

Placing her hands on his chest, she began to ride his cock. Zach lay still, his only movement the occasional squeeze of his fingers on her hips. She had total control over their lovemaking. It made her feel powerful and daring. She could do anything she wanted with Zach…even things she'd yearned to do but never tried with her ex-husband.

"I want you to come inside me."

He ran his hands up her sides and over her breasts. "You won't get any argument from me."

"Then I want you to lick your cum from my pussy."

"You still won't get any argument from me." He lifted his hips, driving his cock farther inside her. "Make me come, Jade."

She rode him hard and fast, tightening her internal muscles as she moved to give him the most pleasure. He groaned deep in his throat while he continued to caress her bouncing breasts. He tugged on her nipples with thumbs and forefingers, making Jade's eyes drift shut in ecstasy.

"No, don't close your eyes. Look at me."

Opening her eyes again took an effort, but Jade managed to do it. His skin now shone with a light coating of perspiration. She slid her hands over his chest and stomach. The crisp hair covering his skin tickled her palms.

"I love touching you," she whispered.

"I love fucking you."

She grinned. "Yeah, that's nice too."

Zach chuckled, then moaned. "Damn it, Jade, I can't laugh and come at the same time."

Her grin widened. "Sorry."

"Yeah, you really sound like you're sorry."

"Do I need to do something special to…bring back the feeling?"

"My feeling is fine. You keep moving that beautiful body."

Jade obeyed his command, lifting her hips until only his head remained inside her, then lowering herself again to take all of his shaft.

"Yeah, like that," he growled. "Move just like that."

No longer lying still, Zach rose to meet her each time she lowered her hips. She soon developed a fast rhythm with him, a rhythm that stole the breath from her lungs. She didn't care. Breathing was highly overrated anyway.

Zach thrust inside her again and again. Another orgasm beckoned, teasing her with its promise of mind-blowing pleasure. Before it could peak, Zach gripped her hips tightly and moaned.

"*Jesus*, Jade!"

His climax took over his entire body. Jade watched, fascinated, as he threw back his head and arched his back. He squeezed his eyes shut and raised his hips off the floor, driving his shaft as far inside her as it would go. She could feel the contractions of his penis as he ejaculated.

What an incredible sight. She loved giving him so much pleasure.

Her own orgasm fizzled, but she didn't mind. She'd had one staggering climax. Knowing Zach had experienced such a powerful orgasm made her happy.

When he opened his eyes, the burning look in them showed her he was far from finished.

She barely had time to inhale before he tugged her to his chest. His next move had her on her back. Holding her head, he kissed her with a savage intensity that made her toes curl.

One more kiss, one more duel of his tongue with hers, and he raised his head. Silently, he withdrew from her body. He dropped a kiss on each nipple, her stomach, the top of each thigh, before he pushed his tongue inside her pussy.

This was no easy build-up, but a full-fledged attack. His tongue flashed over her clit, ran the length of her slit, darted into her ass. Jade bit her bottom lip and inhaled sharply. Grasping her legs behind the knees, she pulled them forward until her knees touched her breasts. Her new position let her see his tongue moving over her intimate flesh. Zach kept up his assault, concentrating on her clit and anus. He pulled her buttocks apart and tongue-fucked her ass.

Jade loved it.

"Stay there, please."

He uttered a soft growl that she took as agreement. One thumb rubbed her clit as he continued driving his tongue into her ass.

"Oh, *yes*! That feels *soooo* good."

The orgasm built quickly, whooshing through her body and making her tremble. She released her legs, letting them fall open while she grabbed Zach's head. Fisting her hands into his thick hair, she rode out the wave.

When she was able to think again, she realized that Zach continued to lick her. She tugged on his hair. "Hey."

He gave her tender clit one more gentle lick before raising his head. "I love making you come."

"I kinda like it too."

"Only 'kinda'?"

"Okay, so I *really* like it."

He nipped the inside of one thigh, then moved up beside her. Lying on his back, he pulled her into his arms. Jade wrapped one arm around his waist. She found the perfect spot on his shoulder to rest her head. Sighing happily, she relaxed against him.

Zach kissed her temple. "You okay?"

"I'm terrific."

"I'll second that." His hand slid up and down her arm in an easy caress. "Whatever reason you and your husband had for divorcing couldn't have been sex. You're an incredible lover."

Jade remained silent for several moments, unsure of how much to say. Zach had told her he wanted to get to know her better. Her ex-husband would be a good place to start.

"Carl found someone else," she said softly.

His arms tightened around her. "He's an idiot."

She shifted her head on his shoulder so she could see his face. "Thank you."

"Just being honest."

Jade rested her head on his shoulder once more. "Carl was—is—a domineering man. Not abusive. He never physically hurt me in any way. But he had strong ideas about how he wanted things done. Several of his ideas and mine didn't…mesh. He wanted me to stay the same young, naïve girl he married. I grew up."

"Most people do."

She slowly ran her hand over his chest and stomach. She did so love touching him. "He found someone fifteen years his junior, someone to hang on his every word and wait on him hand and foot. So he left me. After nineteen years of marriage, he left me."

Zach kissed her temple. "I'm sorry, Jade."

"I was too, at first. I loved Carl, but trying to be who he wanted was…stifling. I've always been a peacemaker. I don't like fighting. Biting my tongue to keep from arguing with him became more difficult."

"So it was a relief when he left you."

That sounded so cold. "I wouldn't call it a *relief*, exactly."

"Are you happier now? Do you like your life without him?"

Jade looked at him. "Yes, I do."

Zach rubbed her back in soft circles. "And you feel guilty about that?"

"I did. I don't anymore. I like who I've become. So does my daughter. She told me yesterday she doesn't want me to ever go back to Carl."

His hand stilled on her back. "Is that a possibility?"

"No. Not at all. I don't love Carl anymore."

She lowered her head again. Content to simply be in Zach's arms, she remained silent. The gentle touch of his hands on her sated body made her totally relax. She sighed and closed her eyes.

"I think you're a fascinating woman, Jade."

Opening her eyes, she propped up on one elbow and looked at him. "Why do you say that?"

"Because it's how I feel. You're beautiful and sexy, but also kind and funny and charming." A crooked grin turned up his lips. "And a bit naughty."

She giggled. "I've never been naughty. It's fun."

"I take it you've never asked a man to lick his cum from your pussy."

Groaning, Jade covered her eyes with one hand. "I can't believe I said that."

"Why?" He pulled her hand away from her face and kissed her palm. "It's what you wanted. There's nothing wrong with telling a man what you want sexually."

"I've never spoken that way, used that kind of language. Breanna tells me I'm an old-fashioned prude."

His gaze passed over her face. "You are most definitely not a prude. There's nothing wrong with being old-fashioned. I've never been impressed with women who say 'fuck' every other word." He squeezed her hand. "Does my saying…graphic words bother you?"

"No. You don't use them except when we're making love or you're teasing me. If you were a total gutter mouth, it would bother me." She shrugged. "See? Hopelessly old-fashioned."

"Hopelessly charming."

His compliment warmed her heart. She smiled. "Thank you."

He tugged on her hand until she leaned over for his kiss. He cradled her head and kissed her softly, breaths barely mingling. His tongue stroked her bottom lip, along the seam of her lips, but gently. It was a kiss of love, not of passion.

Everything inside her melted.

Don't fall for him, Jade, she told herself firmly.

Two kisses later, Jade raised her head. She ran her finger over his lips. He playfully nipped the tip of it. Her heart lurched.

Do not fall for him!

"I rented a DVD while I was out," Zach said. "How about if we watch it while we have our snack?"

"What did you rent?"

"A chick flick." He grinned. "The gal at the video store guaranteed it would make you cry and fall into my arms."

"Sounds perfect."

Ten minutes later, Jade sat on the floor between Zach's legs, her back to his chest. He'd pulled the afghan from the back of the couch and covered them with it. She fed him bites of food with her fingers and he returned the favor while they watched the movie. Such a simple evening, but it felt so right to her.

Zach had money. The car he drove proved that, as did the custom-fit tuxedo. He could be out on the town, blowing money as if he printed it himself. Yet he was here, with her, and seemed to be content to do nothing more exciting than watch a movie while sitting on her floor.

Had she known him only one day? It seemed much longer. He was so in tune with her. He had tons of experience with women, yes, but that didn't mean he'd automatically know what she needed sexually. Women were different in bed with different desires. Some wanted sex slow, some fast, some raunchy. She hadn't told Zach anything, yet he'd known exactly how to please her, how to bring her to orgasm again and again.

Not even years of marriage had given Carl that gift.

"You aren't watching the movie," Zach whispered in her ear.

The brush of his warm breath pebbled her skin with goose bumps. "Sorry."

"What are you thinking?"

She shifted in his arms so she could see his face. "I'm thinking about you."

He smiled. "I like that." His hands slid up from her waist to cup her breasts. "Are you thinking about jumping my bones again?"

Jade laughed. "Not exactly."

"Then what, exactly?"

"I was thinking how in tune we seem to be with each other. You're a fantastic lover. I know you've been with a lot of women, but that doesn't explain how you seem to know *me*. You made love to me as if you've known me forever, as if you knew exactly what pleased me."

"I did." He cradled her jaw in one hand, his thumb caressing her chin. "I don't know how I knew, but I did. Yeah, I've been with a lot of women. It isn't always easy to understand what they need sexually, and some women won't tell me. But with you..." He moved his thumb to her lower lip. "I just *knew*."

Jade stared into those gorgeous blue eyes and her heart swelled. It was too soon. She couldn't be feeling such strong feelings so soon. She couldn't *let* herself feel such strong feelings. Falling in love with Zach would be incredibly stupid.

His thumb dipped inside her lower lip. He picked up the moisture from her mouth and spread it over her lips. "Do you have to work tomorrow?"

Unable to speak with the lump of emotion in her throat, she nodded.

"Any chance you could play hooky?"

"Why?" she croaked.

"I'd like to spend the day with you. I want to show you the house I'm building."

Jade never played hooky. She stayed home if she was sick, but she never blew off work just because she wanted to.

It was time she did exactly that.

"I have a lot of personal time coming to me. I could take the day off."

A slow smile played over his lips. "Does that mean I can spend the night with you again?"

"Don't you have to…work?"

He shook his head. "My time is mine. I want to be with you."

She should tell him no. She should tell him to go home. She should tell him she could never see him again.

Instead, she smiled and said, "I'd like that."

Chapter Fourteen

Jade grabbed the telephone receiver after the first ring. Zach was still sleeping and she didn't want the phone to wake him. "Hello?" she said softly.

"Mom? Why are you whispering?"

Propping the receiver on her shoulder, she returned to the sink to finish filling the coffee carafe. "I'm not whispering."

"Sounds like a whisper to me. Are you okay?"

An image popped into Jade's head, one of Zach spreading creamy dip on her nipples and licking it off. She smiled. "I'm great."

"Then why did your assistant tell me you're sick?"

Jade poured the water into the coffeemaker and pushed the "on" button. "I didn't tell Claire I'm sick. I told her I wouldn't be in today."

"Why not? You *never* miss work. Mom, what's going on?"

"Can't I take a day off without getting bombarded with questions?"

"Not you. When I look up 'workaholic' in the dictionary, I see a picture of you."

"I don't need this abuse before I've had coffee, Bre."

"Okay, okay. I guess even workaholics deserve a day off every now and then. Now, on to the good stuff." Her voice took on a teasing note. "Tell me *all* about your night with Zach."

"Which one?"

Breanna remained silent the length of two heartbeats. "Which *one*?"

Jade grinned. She could picture the confused look on Bre's face. It wasn't often she could pull something on her daughter. "Saturday night, or last night?"

"Ohmigod, he spent *two* nights with you?"

"He did."

"Mom, that's so cool! Now I *really* need details. Was the sex good?"

"Absolutely incredible."

"Is he hung?"

Jade removed a carton of eggs from the refrigerator and placed it on the counter. She pictured Zach on her bed, holding his hard staff in his hand while she lowered herself over it. "If his cock was a measure of intelligence, I'd call him Einstein."

"Mother!"

Jade giggled.

"Mom, you're *giggling*. This is *so* cool! More details."

"Shouldn't you be in class?"

"No classes 'til this afternoon. Don't change the subject! What did he do to you?"

She sighed. "Everything."

"Oh, God, I'm hurting. It's been forever since I've had sex."

"You were going out with what's-his-name two months ago."

"Okay, it's been forever since I've had *good* sex. C'mon, more details. 'Everything' doesn't cut it."

"Breanna, I will not give you a step-by-step description of making love with Zach."

"Why not?"

"Because it's personal."

"Mom, we're not talking about sex with Dad. I'd never ask about that. Kids don't think about their parents having sex. That's an ewwww moment."

Jade chuckled while reaching for a bowl from the cabinet. "It's an ewwww moment with my parents too."

"It's a double ewwww moment to think about my *grandparents* having sex. And you're changing the subject again."

Pausing in the act of cracking an egg into the bowl, Jade let her mind wander over the last day and a half with Zach. She couldn't possibly put into a few words the way he made her feel. "He's a wonderful man, Bre. Charming, kind, funny, considerate, fantastic in bed. He is *so* fantastic in bed. And on the living room floor."

"Not the shower?"

She could hear the amusement in her daughter's voice. "Not yet."

Breanna laughed. "You go, Mom!"

Jade returned the eggs to the refrigerator and removed a block of cheese and plate of sliced ham. She'd decided ham and cheese omelets would be perfect for breakfast. She planned to prepare everything and serve it to Zach in bed.

"I noticed you referred to it as 'making love' and not 'sex'," Breanna said. "Are you falling for him, Mom?"

"Absolutely not." The lie made her stomach clench.

"If he's as wonderful as you say, I don't see how you could help falling for him."

"Breanna, he's ten years younger than me."

"So?"

"So a relationship with him would be impossible."

"Why?"

"He's *young*, Bre. He'll want to get married and have a family someday. I can't give him that family."

"Maybe children aren't important to him. Don't assume anything, Mom. Talk to him about it."

"I've known him two days! And not even two full days—more like…thirty-nine hours."

"So?" Breanna said again. "The amount of time doesn't matter. What matters is the way he makes you feel. How does he make you feel?"

Jade paused in the act of removing a wire whisk from the utensil drawer. "He makes me feel good about myself," she said softly. "He makes me feel attractive and sexy. I'm not a chubby divorcee to him. I'm a woman he wants to be with, a woman he wants to please. He makes me feel…"

She stopped when the tiny hairs on the back of her neck stood up. Slowly, she turned. Zach stood in the doorway, leaning on the frame.

He was gloriously nude.

Zach smiled to himself at the stricken expression in Jade's eyes. He'd caught her talking about him. Although he'd only heard her last four sentences, he liked what he'd heard. He liked knowing he'd given her self-esteem a boost.

He sauntered toward her. Her gaze moved down his body to his groin. As if on cue, his cock began to harden.

"Your daughter?" he mouthed when he stood in front of her.

She nodded.

Zach took the receiver from her limp fingers. "Good morning, Breanna," he said, his gaze locked with Jade's.

"Good morning, Zach."

"You don't mind if I hang up now, do you? I want to ravish your mother."

Breanna giggled. "Go for it."

Zach pushed the "off" button and laid the telephone on the counter. "Good morning, Jade."

"Good morning," she whispered.

Tunneling his fingers into her hair, he tilted her head to the exact position he wanted and kissed her. She immediately relaxed and parted her lips for the thrust of his tongue. He kissed her slow and deep, the way he'd learned she liked.

She purred.

That sound shot straight to his shaft. With his lips still pressed to hers, he wrapped one arm around her waist and lifted her. He turned and set her on the large butcher-block table in the middle of the kitchen. Before she had the chance to pull away from him, he clasped the back of her head with one hand and held her still while he devoured her mouth.

God, he loved kissing her.

Using his free hand, Zach jerked her silky robe off one shoulder until her breast was bared. He cupped the full mound and ran his thumb over the jutting nipple. Jade whimpered. Still kissing her, he kneaded her firm flesh…lifting, squeezing, tugging on the hard nub. Her breathing grew heavier, her kisses more frantic. She wrapped her legs around his waist and hunched into his pelvis.

He needed to fuck her, but not yet. Not until she'd come at least once. He clasped her hips and pulled her to the very edge of the table. Pushing her thighs far apart, he leaned over and buried his tongue in her pussy.

"Zach!"

She came almost instantly. Zach pushed two fingers inside her and felt her contractions clench around them. Once wasn't enough for him. He continued to pump his fingers in and out of her body as he licked her clit.

When the contractions from her second orgasm stopped gripping his fingers, Zach stood and thrust inside her.

Jade reclined on the table, her eyes closed and her fists tightly clenched at her sides. Her robe remained tied at the waist, but hung open to expose those beautiful breasts. He pushed the lapels wide and cradled the heavy globes.

"I love your body," he said huskily.

She opened her eyes and looked at him. "I love what you do to my body."

"How about if I keep on doing it?"

"Oh, yesssssss."

Zach increased the speed of his thrusts. He slipped his hands beneath her buttocks and lifted, letting him drive deeper into her pussy. Jade cupped her breasts, caressing and twisting her nipples. The sight of her pleasuring herself sent him over the top. The orgasm slithered down his spine and grabbed his balls. He dug his fingers into Jade's hips and groaned out his release.

Zach had to lean against the table since his legs felt like overcooked noodles. When he was certain he could stand on his own, he tugged Jade to a sitting position. "Wrap your arms and legs around me."

She did as he said. He lifted her from the table and carried her from the kitchen.

Directly into the shower.

He leaned over and turned on the faucet. Warm water sluiced over them.

"Zach, my robe!"

"It's washable, isn't it?"

"Yes, but I usually wash it in the washing machine, not the shower."

He grinned. "So be different today."

She laughed. "You're a nut."

"Guilty as charged." He stepped to the side until Jade's back touched the wall. "I'm a nut for you."

He shifted his hips, and she gasped. "How can you still be hard?"

"Good metabolism."

She chuckled, but it quickly turned to a moan. "I can't believe how deep you get."

He drew his cock out to the head, then thrust inside her again. "Believe it."

Water cascaded over Zach's back as he leisurely fucked her. His first orgasm had left him satisfied, so he was in no hurry for a second one. He'd rather concentrate on Jade and what she needed.

The sound of her breath catching made him pick up the pace. She clutched his shoulders. She nipped his neck. Her fingernails dug into his back. Zach knew those were all signs she was about to come again.

Jade arched her neck and groaned. Two more thrusts and he followed her.

Zach didn't move for several moments. He leaned heavily against Jade's body, afraid his knees would buckle and he'd drop her. "Intense" didn't begin to describe the orgasm he'd just experienced.

"Oh, yes," Jade whispered. "Fantastic in the shower too."

He lifted his head from her shoulder and looked at her. "What?"

"Nothing."

Zach strongly suspected her comment had something to do with her earlier conversation with Breanna. "Were you and your daughter talking about our lovemaking?"

A lovely blush bloomed in her cheeks. "Maybe a little."

"You told her I'm fantastic?"

She ran her fingers into his wet hair. "Oh, yes."

He smiled. "Fantastic is a good description. I like that."

"It's the truth. I don't think I had as many orgasms in nineteen years of marriage as I've had with you."

"Mmm, and we still have the rest of the day…and night."

"Oh, my God, I'll never survive."

"There's always mouth-to-mouth resuscitation."

Jade smiled wickedly. "There is that."

Zach chuckled. He liked when her naughty side surfaced. "For now, I think we should get this robe off of you and finish our shower." The sound of Jade's stomach rumbling made him chuckle again. "And feed you."

"I was about to cook breakfast when *someone* ravished me."

"Are you complaining?"

"You think I'm crazy? I'll never complain when you ravish me."

"That's what I like to hear."

* * * * *

Jade slowly wandered into the next room. Zach had completed the outside walls of his house, the roof, and the studs that divided each room. It appeared he was currently working on the electrical. Numerous wires hung from the ceiling and snaked down the studs. "Guest room?" she guessed.

He nodded. "I have two, in case my brother and sister want to stay over at the same time."

She stepped through the doorway into the next room. "Which room is this?"

"My computer room."

"I'm a little confused about the directions. Do the windows face west?"

"Yes. I like to watch the sunsets." He gestured toward an opening to their right. "My bedroom connects to it. I wanted a separate room for my computer and files, but still convenient to get to."

Jade walked into his bedroom. She'd never been a good judge of size or distance, but it looked huge. "How big is this?"

"Almost six hundred square feet. The house is close to three thousand square feet."

"Why so big for a single guy?"

Zach shrugged. "Because I wanted it and I can afford it, especially since I'm doing the majority of the work myself." He slipped his hands in the back pockets of his jeans. "I may have gone a bit overboard in here, but I have a king-sized bed. I plan to have a large entertainment center on the south wall. Plus, that square footage includes the walk-in closet."

"I certainly love my walk-in closet. That and the kitchen are what sold me on the house."

"That isn't the house you lived in with your husband?"

"No. We sold that when we divorced and divided the profit." All this talk of size and features gave Jade the perfect opportunity to dig a little deeper. "It's a great house for a family."

"I guess. I hadn't thought of that."

"Don't you want to have a family?"

"Maybe, with the right woman."

Jade swallowed. She definitely was *not* the right woman for that.

He removed his hands from his pockets and walked toward her. "I honestly haven't thought about children of my own, Jade. I come from a large family. I have three uncles on my dad's side and four aunts on my mom's side and they all have kids." He stopped in front of her. "I love my cousins, but I don't know if I'm dad material."

"You're a sensitive, caring man, Zach. You'll be a wonderful father."

"I'm not in any hurry." He cradled her neck in one hand. "I always wear a condom, Jade. Common sense demands it, both for protection and birth control. I didn't use one with you last night or this morning." He caressed her cheek with his thumb. "I'm clean. All our escorts have regular physicals and blood work. We insist on it."

"I haven't been with a man in two years."

"I know that, but what about birth control? Are you on the Pill?"

"No."

"I'll admit I'm not up-to-date on all the birth control methods available now. What are you using?"

"Nothing." She touched his hand, pressing it closer to her. "I can't have any more children, Zach. I had several ovarian cysts over a period of years. They were all benign, but my doctor suggested I have a hysterectomy when I was twenty-seven. I did."

"I saw the faded scar, so knew you had some kind of surgery." He gave her a crooked grin. "I've studied your body the past few days."

His joke made her smile. "You have been rather…up close and personal."

"I've loved every second of it."

"So have I."

He kissed her, slowly and thoroughly. Jade's toes curled inside her shoes while her heart clenched in her chest. This would be their last night together. The thought of never seeing Zach again was more painful than if someone jabbed a knife into her. But she had no choice. This conversation about family and children proved that.

Zach ended the kiss and took her in his arms. Jade went willingly, wrapping her arms tightly around his neck. She wanted every second of time with him she could get before she had to tell him goodbye.

"I'm falling in love with you, Jade," he whispered.

His words froze her for several seconds. Slowly, she unwrapped her arms from around his neck and leaned back so she could see his face. "What?" she asked weakly.

"I'm falling in love with you."

"But-but you *can't*."

His eyebrows drew together in a frown. "I *can't*?"

"No. Zach, I'm ten years older than you."

"You have a weird hang-up about age, Jade."

She pulled away from him and took two steps backward. She could think more clearly when he wasn't touching her. "I just told you I can't have children. Even if I could, I don't want to. I'm almost forty. I certainly don't want to become a mother again at my age. I'm content to wait for grandchildren."

"And I just told you I'm in no hurry to be a father. I don't know if I even *want* to be a father. I don't have a burning desire to see a miniature version of me running around." He took her hand and raised it to his mouth. He ran his tongue between her fingers while he held her gaze. "I want to be with you. That's all I care about."

Jade's heart began to pound. This man stood before her, a man so handsome and sexy that he almost seemed unreal, telling her he wanted to be with her. She wanted to be with him too, but how? It wouldn't be fair to him for them to continue their relationship, knowing there was a good chance he'd change his mind about having his own children someday. She would never stand in the way of him becoming a father.

"Give us a chance, Jade."

Grasping at anything she could to keep from weakening under his intense blue gaze, she asked, "What about your…job?"

"I have no job, at least not as an escort. The business belongs to my brother, sister, and me. I'll recruit new escorts. I'll do paperwork. I'll help Michelle with the yard work if she wants. I won't be intimate with any other woman. I only want to be with you." He gestured around the room with his free hand. "*This* is my main job now—building my house." He kissed her palm. "I hope I can call it *our* house someday."

Jade groaned. "You aren't making this easy."

He grinned devilishly. "Good." With one tug, she was back in his arms. "I've made a very good living with Coopers' Companions and most of what I've earned is in the bank. I wouldn't have any problem supporting us."

"You're moving *way* too fast."

"I move fast when something is important to me." He ran his hands up and down her spine. "Spend time with me. Let me show you how good we can be together."

"You've already shown me how good we can be together."

"I'm not talking sexually, although I'll admit I intend for the sex to continue at every opportunity."

"Thank goodness."

Zach chuckled, but quickly became serious again. "The first time I saw you, walking down your hallway toward me, I forgot to breathe. That's never happened to me. There isn't a doubt in my mind or heart how I feel about you." He kissed her gently. "A chance, Jade. Give us a chance."

She could do that. She could spend more time with him, see if it might really be possible to have a future together.

She wanted it to be possible.

"We could give it a try and see what happens."

Zach smiled. "That's all I ask."

Chapter Fifteen

&

Zach stepped through the entrance to Coopers' Companions whistling "I Can't Get No Satisfaction". The song had worked well for him one week ago. He saw no reason to change now.

He'd found out seven days ago today that he would be Jade's escort to her hospital's gala. His life had completely changed since then. He'd been happy being an escort, but no more. He didn't want any other woman but Jade.

God, he loved her. Waking up with her in his arms this morning had felt so right. He could hardly wait until they made it permanent. He didn't want to spend one night without her.

"Where the *hell* have you been?"

Brent's roar made Zach turn. His brother stood in the doorway to the office, a ferocious scowl on his face. "Good morning to you, too, Brent."

"Don't give me that 'good morning' shit. I've been trying to call you for two days. I've left half a dozen voice mails on your cell. Why haven't you called me back?"

Zach passed his brother and walked into the office. "I've been busy."

"Too busy to check your messages?"

"I took the weekend off." He flopped down in one of the two chairs before the desk. "Haven't you ever taken a weekend off?"

"No."

"I guess I'm not as dedicated as you."

Still scowling, Brent sat in his own chair and reached for a stack of papers on top of the desk. "I'll let it slide this time."

"You'll *let it slide*? Who's the oldest here, Brent?"

"Age has nothing to do with this, Zach. We're running a business. You don't 'take the weekend off' without checking in." He fanned the papers in his hands. "I could've set you up both Sunday night and last night. I had to send Rod in your place."

"We've never gotten any complaints about Rod."

"Yeah, but it should've been *you*, Zach."

"I can't go on every date. I've slacked off lately since I've been working on my house. You know that."

Brent frowned. "Yeah, I know that. But you are the escort most requested, the one who's built our reputation." He shook the papers toward Zach. "I've already taken twenty-five calls this morning from women who need an escort this weekend. We only have fifteen guys, counting you and me." He slapped the papers back down on the desk. "I knew we should've hired more escorts months ago."

"However many you think we need to hire, add one more. I'm quitting."

The stunned look on Brent's face would've made Zach laugh if this wasn't such a serious matter. Brent's mouth opened and closed, then opened and closed again as if he didn't know what to say.

"You're what?"

"You heard me. I said it quite clearly."

Brent chuckled. His chuckle turned into boisterous laughter. Zach waited, his temper slowly rising, while his brother guffawed.

"That's good, Zach." Brent wiped his eyes. "I needed a good laugh."

"I'm not joking. I am no longer an escort as of this minute."

Brent's laughter abruptly died. "What the hell are you talking about?"

"I'm talking about quitting. I'm talking about having a life of my own with one woman."

"Wait a minute, wait a minute." He held up his hand, palm out. "What one woman?"

"Jade Talmage."

Brent's eyes widened and his mouth slackened. "Jade Talmage? The old broad you took out Saturday night?"

Zach clenched his hands into fists on the arms of his chair. "Jade is not old, and she's not a broad. I highly suggest you watch your mouth, little brother."

"My God, Zach, she's almost *forty*! What did she do to you? She couldn't have been that hot a fuck."

"Yeah, she was that hot, but it isn't just sex, Brent. She's charming and lovely and fun to be with—"

"You sound like you're spouting lines from some 1950s romance novel! Grow up, Zach."

"*You're* a fine one to tell *me* to grow up. You can't see past a woman's pussy. I see *everything* about Jade, and I like what I see."

"The next thing you'll say is you *looooove* her," Brent said with a snarl.

"I *do* love her."

"Christ!" Brent surged to his feet. Placing his palms flat on the desk, he leaned forward and glared at Zach. "This is insane! You can't leave the business for one woman."

"I'm not leaving the business. I'll still work in any way you or Michelle need me to. But I won't be an escort. I won't cheat on Jade."

"*You're* the one the ladies ask for! They all want a piece of that big dick you carry between your legs. Apparently, so does Jade Talmage."

"*That's enough*!" Zach stood also and returned his brother's glare. "Watch your mouth, Brent."

"Or what? I see your clenched fists. You gonna hit me, big brother?"

"Don't push me."

"Hey," Michelle said from the doorway. "I could hear y'all outside. What's going on?"

"Your brother is a fucking fool." Brent threw the comment over his shoulder as he brushed past Michelle and out the door.

Michelle watched him leave, wincing when the front door slammed. She looked at Zach. "You want to explain what happened here?"

Zach adored his sister. He figured Brent was a big boy and would get over his temper tantrum. Zach didn't want to hurt Michelle in any way. "Sit down with me, Chelle. I want to talk to you."

"Sounds serious."

"Yeah, it is."

Zach followed Michelle the short distance across the room to the loveseat. He waited until she sat, then sat beside her. Leaning forward, he clasped his hands together between his thighs as he tried to figure out how to tell her about Jade. "Brent and I had a difference of opinion on something."

"You and Brent had a fight. That's a lot more than a difference of opinion."

"Yeah, well, you know how Brent is. He flies off the handle over everything." Zach shifted on the loveseat and cleared his throat. "Chelle, I'm no longer an escort as of this morning."

The confused look on his sister's face didn't surprise Zach. While Michelle didn't know any intimate details about his dates, he and Brent both teased her about sex. They liked to watch her blush. "You've quit? Why?" A look of fear filled her eyes. She grabbed his forearm. "You aren't sick, are you?"

"No, no, nothing like that." He laid his hand over hers and squeezed. "I promise I'm fine."

"Then I don't understand."

"I've met someone, Chelle. I was her escort Saturday night and I... Well, I fell for her hard and fast. I don't want to be with any other women. I only want Jade."

Michelle blew out a breath. "Wow. This is really sudden, Zach. Are you sure?"

"Very sure. I love her, Chelle."

She clasped her hands together in her lap. Zach recognized that signal. She was about to turn on her "mother-mode".

"I heard some of what you and Brent said. I have no idea about your...physical endowments, and I certainly do *not* want to know. That would be *way* too much information. But I do know we've built this business mostly because of you. Brent is business-minded and an organizer. You're a natural charmer. The women love you, and they ask for you again and again. Can you really give that up?"

"I'm a third of this company, Michelle. I'll still work here, in whatever capacity you, Brent, and I decide. Maybe you can even teach me that spreadsheet program you use."

She wrinkled her nose. "You're completely hopeless on a computer, you know that."

Zach spread his arms. "So I'll interview prospective escorts, or mow the lawn, or cook. I'll do *something* useful."

"I just hope mowing the lawn will be enough for you."

"I'll get all the sex I need from Jade."

She blushed, which was exactly what he wanted. "You're getting into that too much information territory, Zach."

"Sorry." He kissed her cheek. "I love to tease you."

"Yeah, I know. You don't have to love it *quite* so much." She pushed a lock of her brown hair behind one ear. "Why is it you and Brent can make me blush so easily? I don't have this problem on dates."

"Because we're your brothers and know which buttons to push. And don't mention your dates. That would be TMI territory for me. Thinking about my baby sister having sex makes me cringe."

Michelle grinned wickedly. "Want details about David? He's really—"

"No, I don't want any details about your current beau, or any others."

"Hey, working with a bunch of hunky guys whom I can't touch isn't easy on a gal."

He'd never thought of it that way. Coopers' Companions had no rule written in stone, but Michelle had insisted a long time ago that she wouldn't ever get involved with one of the escorts. She was a young, healthy, attractive woman. Being around all the testosterone in this place had to be frustrating at times.

Michelle squeezed his hand. "If you love her, *really* love her, then go for it. Brent will get over his snit in time."

"I really love her, Chelle."

"That's good enough for me." She stood and tugged Zach to his feet. "Get out of here. Go plan a special dinner for the two of you. You're an incredible cook. Wine and dine her, then spend the rest of the night in her arms."

"I'm not seeing her tonight. She has to work late."

"Then plan it for tomorrow. Surprise her with your beef stroganoff. If she doesn't already love you, that'll clinch it."

Zach had never invited a woman to his condo. He wanted to invite Jade there. He'd cook dinner for them, then they'd soak in his hot tub. After that, he'd give her a full-body massage before they made love.

He liked that idea. He liked it a lot.

Smiling, Zach kissed his sister's cheek. "Thanks, Chelle. Beef stroganoff it is."

* * * * *

Movement in the doorway drew Jade's attention away from the financial updates scattered across her desk. Doug Lassiter entered her office, closing the door behind him.

The head of surgery did not come to her office. Jade immediately became wary. "Hello, Doug."

"Good afternoon, Jade."

Ignoring the two upholstered chairs that sat in front of her desk, he rounded her desk and propped one hip on the corner. The position drew his pants tight across his groin.

She really didn't like him being here. Unsure what to do, she remained silent, waiting for him to speak again.

"I wanted to congratulate you on the gala. You did an outstanding job."

"Thank you," she said, confused. Doug Lassiter rarely said hello to her, much less paid her a compliment.

"Everyone had a good time." His gaze dipped to her breasts. "Especially you, apparently."

Every cell in her body went on alert. "I beg your pardon?"

"That dress you wore was very sexy, Jade. And your…date. He was young enough to be your…nephew."

Jade bristled at his rudeness. "I see no reason for this conversation, Dr. Lassiter."

"Then let me clarify what I'm saying and get right to the point. The board wasn't happy with the way you conducted yourself at the gala, Jade. Flaunting your body and your young man was totally inappropriate."

This man had—as Zach put it—humped her on the dance floor, or tried to. He had a lot of nerve to call her behavior inappropriate. Attempting to rein in her escalating temper, Jade slowly laid down her pen and sat back in her chair. "I don't recall when the board made you its spokesman."

"I'm the head of surgery. I'm in close contact with the board members. I know how they think."

"So now you're a mind reader?"

His eyes narrowed, his lips thinned. "I wouldn't be so quick to pop off at me if I were you. I have the power to have you fired."

Unfortunately, that could be true. Doug Lassiter had a lot of clout with the board and the hospital administrator. "So what, exactly, are you saying to me, Doug?"

"I'm saying I'll do everything I can to help you keep your job, despite your lack of judgment."

"In return for?"

His gaze dipped to her breasts again and lingered there. "I'm sure we can work out something."

Jade would've laughed if she hadn't been so angry. This man was actually suggesting she have sex with him in exchange for keeping her job. "It's time for you to leave, Dr. Lassiter."

"Oh, come on, Jade. We're both adults. The way you dressed, along with that young stud you brought with you, practically shouted that you're hot for sex." He leaned forward and ran one forefinger down her cheek. "I can give you anything you need."

She had to catch herself before she jerked away from him. She needed to find out exactly how far he planned to take this ridiculous farce. "You seem to have forgotten you have a wife."

"My wife is the least of your worries."

"Actually, I think she's very important. I don't believe she'll appreciate the sexual harassment charge I file against you."

He looked stunned for a moment, then burst out laughing. "You wouldn't file on me. Who do you think the board will support—you or me?"

The board would more than likely support the hospital's star surgeon, but Jade wouldn't admit that to Doug. "I asked you to leave, doctor. Now I'm demanding it."

The laughter abruptly died in his eyes. Doug straightened the cuffs of his perfectly pressed, pale blue shirt before he stood. "I'll give you a few days to think about it, Jade. It would be in your best interest to reconsider."

Not believing his comment deserved a response, Jade remained silent. She sat still and watched Doug Lassiter stroll out of her office.

Once he left, Jade picked up her pen and threw it across the room. It bounced off the wall and fell with a clatter to the tile floor. How *dare* he? Doug Lassiter had barely spoken to her in the three years he'd been at this hospital. Now, because of a daring dress and a date with a younger man, he assumed he could blackmail her into having sex with him.

He wasn't the only one who'd given her a hard time today. She'd received "friendly" teasing from several coworkers about the hunk she'd taken to the gala. One nurse—a woman Jade had never liked—had outright asked if

Zach was as hot in bed as he was on the dance floor. Refusing to answer her rude question, Jade had simply walked away.

She wouldn't let the teasing bother her, and she certainly wouldn't let Doug Lassiter get under her skin. His threats didn't frighten her. No one from the board had approached her all day. Surely someone would have contacted her if she were truly in danger of losing her job.

Jade had declined to see Zach tonight, telling him she had to catch up on the work she'd neglected yesterday. Now she wished she'd agreed to go out with him. She longed to be with him right now.

Getting any additional work done today would be impossible. Jade began to straighten up her desk. A glass of wine and a long soak in the bathtub would do nicely tonight. Tomorrow, she'd see Zach again.

Jade paused with her hand on her purse. She didn't want to wait until tomorrow. She wanted to be with Zach tonight.

Digging her cell phone from the bottom of her purse, she quickly punched in Zach's number that she'd already memorized.

"Hey, lady," he answered in a deep, smooth voice.

Jade shivered as goose bumps skittered up her spine. Just the sound of his voice turned her on. "Hey, yourself. What are you doing?"

"Playing with myself and thinking of you."

She smiled. "How would you like to play with me instead?"

"Mmm, love to, but you said you have to work late."

"I changed my mind. Would you like to come over for supper?"

"I have a better idea. How about if you come to my place and I'll cook supper for you? Then we can soak in my hot tub."

"Naked?"

"Of course."

"Goody."

He chuckled. "After that, I'll have a surprise for you."

"Does it involve chocolate body paint?"

"It can."

"How long will it take me to get there from here?"

"About thirty minutes."

Jade grabbed a pen and scratch pad from her desk. "What's your address?"

Chapter Sixteen

ჯ

It took Jade thirty-five minutes to drive to Zach's condo. Luckily, she'd left work shortly after three, so she missed the start of the heavy rush-hour traffic. She parked her car in a visitor's space close to the entrance.

He opened the door before she had the chance to ring the bell, wearing only a pair of low-rise faded jeans. "Hi," he said with a smile.

"Hi. Were you watching for me?"

"Absolutely." Taking her hand, he tugged her past the entrance, shut the door, and pushed her back against it. "I've been counting the minutes until I could kiss you."

Jade laughed, but her laughter was soon cut off by his kiss. She sighed to herself as he nipped at her lips. He soothed the nips with his tongue before sending it deep into her mouth. He kissed her over and over, as if he'd be happy to stand right here with her pressed against the door and kiss her for hours.

That worked for her.

She wrapped her arms around him and returned every kiss, until the need for air made her pull away from him.

"Wow," she breathed.

"I'll second that." Zach sounded as out of breath as she. He leaned his forehead against hers and closed his eyes. "I love kissing you."

"I love it, too."

He opened his eyes again and gazed into hers. Running his hands down her back, he squeezed her buttocks. "It's too early for me to cook supper. Would you like to soak in the hot tub first?"

"That sounds wonderful."

He kissed the tip of her nose. "I'll show you the way. You can get undressed while I fix us a drink. Deal?"

"Deal."

Zach led the way through his spacious living room to a set of French doors that opened onto a covered patio. Jade took in everything as she passed it, noting the overstuffed furniture and simple furnishings. The masculine décor practically screamed "professional interior designer". The condo was beautiful, but she couldn't help thinking a woman's touch would make it more eye-pleasing.

She forgot about the inside when she stepped through the French doors. The hot tub was surrounded by lush green plants. They made her believe she stood in the middle of the jungle. She wouldn't have been surprised to see a brightly colored parrot swoop down from the top of the tallest plant.

"Zach, this is incredible."

"Thanks. I wanted a place to totally relax and forget all the stress for a while. Michelle helped me come up with this. Some people have a green thumb. She has ten."

"It's perfect."

He touched a button on the lip of the tub. Pale blue lights came on in the bottom. The next button he pushed started the jets churning. Jade already felt calmer just thinking about being surrounded by the warm, bubbling water.

"Make yourself comfortable. I'll be right back with our drinks."

Quickly shedding her sensible suit and the rest of her working outfit, Jade climbed naked into the foamy water. She sighed as she tilted her head back and settled into a corner of the four-person hot tub. Shifting slightly, she located a jet that would pulse directly into the small of her back. Heaven.

"You look good in there."

Jade lowered her head and looked at Zach. He stood next to the tub, a crooked smile on his lips, holding two glasses of something frothy and dark pink. "I could get really spoiled to this."

"I'll have a bigger tub at my house. And an outside pool. All the better to spoil you." He held out one glass to her.

"It makes no sense to me why some woman hasn't already snatched you up."

"I was waiting for the right one." His gaze dipped to her breasts. She knew they were half exposed by her position. She did nothing to hide them from him. His smile widened. "I finally found her."

He clinked his glass against hers and sipped his drink. Jade drank from her own glass. The taste of strawberries exploded on her tongue. "Hmm, good. Strawberry daiquiri?"

"My specialty."

She drank again, enjoying the cool liquid sliding over her tongue and down her throat. "It most certainly is. This is wonderful."

She watched him as he drank again. Seeing him in the tight, faded jeans was a definite turn-on, but she wanted to feel his slick, wet skin against hers. "I think," she said after setting her glass on the lip of the tub, "one of us is overdressed."

"You must mean me."

"I do."

"I'm only wearing jeans. Not even any shorts."

The outline of his cock through the denim proved that fact. "Show me."

He set his glass next to hers. She watched his fingers while he unsnapped his jeans. The outline of his cock grew more pronounced as he slid down the zipper. She saw dark pubic hair before his glorious shaft came into view. Once free of the tight denim, his penis sprang up against his belly.

Jade swallowed.

"Like what you see?"

She licked her lips. "Very much." Her gaze shifted from his shaft to his eyes and back again. "I'd like it better if I could touch it." Giving him her best seductive smile, she patted the lip of the tub next to her. "Sit right here and let me play a bit."

Zach climbed over the lip and sat down, legs spread wide. "You can play with me any way you want to."

"I love a man who's easy."

Jade moved between his legs. For a moment, she simply absorbed the sight of him. Some women didn't find the nude male body attractive. Jade did. She especially enjoyed looking at him when he was aroused—like now—but also when his cock was relaxed. Zach liked to be naked, and took every opportunity to ignore clothes. Watching him walk around naked gave her pleasure. *Everything* about him gave her pleasure.

Scooping up water in both hands, she let it dribble over his shaft. Zach sucked in a sharp breath as if the warm water had burned him. "Is this all right?"

"Yeah." His voice sounded choked. He cleared his throat. "It feels good."

"I like making you feel good." She dribbled more water over his cock, then circled the head with her tongue. "Do you have any requests?"

He arched his hips toward her. "Suck me. But not long enough to make me come. I want to be deep inside you when I come."

His words made her clit throb. "So I can lick and suck as long as I want, but I can't let you come?"

"Oh, yeah," he rasped. "As long as you want."

"Sounds like a deal to me."

Jade proceeded to make love to his shaft with her mouth—long, slow licks with her tongue, teasing nips with her teeth, gentle suction on the head. When Zach would pump his hips as if he were really getting into the feeling, she'd stop and let him relax a moment, then start all over again.

Several moments passed before he cupped her chin and pulled her mouth away from him. "That's enough." His words were choppy from his heavy breathing. "One more lick and I'll come."

"Do we get to trade places now?"

Zach chuckled. "Ready for some tongue action?"

"Definitely."

"I'll be more than happy to lick on that pretty pussy, but there's something else I want to do first."

He rose from the tub. Opening a cabinet on the wall, he removed two large blue towels.

"Aren't you getting in here with me?"

He shook his head. "I have other plans. Dry off and come with me."

Jade grinned wickedly at his choice of words. "I love coming with you."

He chuckled. "Hussy."

"And you love that I am."

"Oh, yeah."

Jade climbed from the tub. Their teasing banter had made Zach's erection relax a bit. Seeing the water running off her nude body brought it back in an instant. She'd brought him to the brink of release over and over with her mouth. Ignoring his body's needs wouldn't be easy while he gave Jade her massage.

He picked up both their glasses and led the way to his bedroom. He'd already pulled back the bedspread so she could lie on the sheets. The bottle of massage oil sat on his nightstand. Setting down the glasses next to the bottle, he picked up the remote control for his CD player. One press of the "play" button and soft music filled the room.

Her eyes were shining with pleasure when he looked at her again. "Does that bottle of oil mean what I think it means?"

"It does. Lie down on your stomach and get comfortable. I'm going to give you the best massage you've ever had."

Jade kissed him before following his direction. Once she lay on the bed, one pillow under her head and one under her stomach, Zach straddled her hips. Picking up the bottle of oil, he poured a generous amount into his palm. On impulse, he also dribbled a stream between her buttocks.

Jade shifted on the bed. "That tickles."

"Not for long." He spread the oil around her anus with his thumb. "Still tickle?"

She shifted again, raising her buttocks as if asking for more. "No."

"You like it when I touch you here, don't you?"

"Yes."

"Finger or tongue, you like it, don't you?"

"Yessss."

He continued to caress her with his thumb. "Do you like anal sex, Jade?"

"I…don't know. Carl never… Mmm, that's *nice*. He never did that to me."

"Did you want him to?"

"I…thought about it."

Zach's cock jerked into full erection again when he thought of being inside that beautiful ass. "Did you know a woman can come from having her anus stimulated?"

"I've read that, but I've never…" Her voice trailed off in a moan when he began rubbing harder. "That feels *really* good. Ah! Zach, *please*."

He rubbed harder, faster. "Please what?"

"Please keep on… Just like that. Oh, *yes*!"

Her body shuddered. Unable to wait any longer for his own climax, Zach used the oil still in his palm to lubricate his cock. "I want to fuck your ass, Jade. Do you want to try it?"

Her hands clenched into fists on the pillow. "Yes."

Holding his shaft with one hand, he slowly guided the head inside her ass. Jade tightened her buttocks.

"Relax, babe. I won't hurt you."

Her back rose and fell with a deep breath. Zach waited a moment while she relaxed internal muscles, then pushed his cock another inch farther inside her. He heard Jade moan softly. She lifted her hips toward him.

"Okay so far?"

"Yes. Oh, yes."

He smiled at the breathless sound of her voice. He continued to push his shaft into her ass, until he was all the way inside her.

Jade moaned. So did Zach.

"You still okay?" he asked.

"It feels… I never suspected it could feel so incredible."

He pulled back until only the head remained inside, then thrust forward again. Jade reached back and pulled her buttocks apart.

"That's the way. Show me you want to be fucked."

"I do. Harder, please."

Zach leaned forward so he could rest his hands on the bed on either side of Jade. "God, this looks so good. I wish you could see my cock in your ass." He increased the speed of his thrusts slowly, wanting to make sure she was truly ready for him.

"Harder!"

He continued to build up speed, until he pounded his cock into her ass. She lifted her hips, meeting every thrust. The pressure built in his balls.

"Zach!"

Her anus contracted around his cock as she came. He pushed his shaft in to the balls, squeezed his eyes shut, and let his orgasm overtake him.

He saw stars. His arms gave out on him and he collapsed on top of Jade's back. A gentle "ooph" from her made him prop up on his elbows.

"I'm sorry," he said into her ear. "I didn't mean to squash you."

"Did you squash me? I'm breathing…too hard to…notice."

Zach chuckled and raked his teeth over her earlobe. "I got a little sidetracked. I brought you in here for a massage, I swear."

"Do you hear one word of complaint from me?"

"No." His tongue dipped inside her ear. "Did you like it?"

"You have to ask?"

"Just making sure, 'cause I promise you I'll want to do it again. Soon."

"Tonight?"

"Maybe." He tugged her earlobe between his teeth. "You like my cock in your ass?"

"Love it. The feeling of fullness is incredible."

"I love how free you are with me, how you're willing to try new things. You're an incredibly sexy lady."

"You make me want to try new things. I feel like I can do anything with you."

"You can. Anything, anytime, anywhere. I'll do anything you want sexually."

Zach slowly pulled his cock from her ass. Jade moaned softly.

"Okay, sweetheart?"

She nodded.

"Ready for your massage?"

"After two orgasms, I can't promise you how long I'll stay awake if you give me a massage."

He kissed her between her shoulder blades. "If you fall asleep, I'll wake you when I have supper ready."

Jade adjusted her head on the pillow to a more comfortable position. What a considerate guy. It amazed her that he'd reached the age of thirty without becoming involved with a woman. He'd told her he'd been waiting for the right one. How lucky that he considered her to be the right woman for him.

She closed her eyes when his oiled hands touched her shoulders. A soak in the hot tub, half a strawberry daiquiri, and two powerful orgasms left her body completely limp. Falling asleep wouldn't be at all difficult.

"You asleep yet?" Zach whispered.

"Close." She sighed. "This is wonderful. I really needed this after my run-in with Doug Lassiter."

His thumbs pressed into her shoulder blades. "You had a run-in with Doug Lassiter?"

"Mmm-hmm. He's such a jerk."

"What did he do?"

Jade swallowed. Her tongue felt thick. She'd be asleep in another few seconds. "He tried to blackmail me into having sex with him."

"What?"

Jerked awake by the tone of his voice, Jade turned her head so she could see Zach. Fire flashed in his eyes.

"Did that bastard touch you?"

"Just-just my cheek."

"I'll kill him."

Jade knew that statement was a figure of speech, that people often said they'd kill someone when they were very angry. The stormy look in Zach's eyes made her believe he was serious. She rolled to her side. "Zach, it's fine. I took care of it."

"What did he say to you?"

"He said the board wasn't happy with the gown I wore to the gala. He offered to smooth things over with the members if I'd have sex with him."

"Did anyone from the board actually say something to you about your dress?"

"No."

Zach's hands clenched into fists. "No one threatens you, Jade. I don't care if that jackass is the head of surgery at your hospital, *no one* threatens you."

Jade sat up and took his hands. "Doug Lassiter can't do anything to hurt me, I promise."

He pushed his hair back from his forehead. "I knew I should've decked the son of a bitch Saturday night."

"Yeah, you probably should have." She wrapped her arms around his neck and hugged him. "I appreciate you trying to protect me."

He returned her fierce hug. "I love you. I'll protect you with my life."

Love for him bloomed in her heart. Falling in love so deeply so quickly didn't seem possible, yet she had. No matter how much teasing she received from her coworkers, or the harassment from Doug Lassiter, being with Zach would make it all worth it.

Everything would be wonderful for them from now on.

Chapter Seventeen

ꟹ

Jade absently swished her straw through her Dr Pepper. She tried to stay focused on her conversation with Breanna, but her mind kept wandering. Over and over, she thought about what had happened two days ago at Ridgmar Mall…

A hand waving in front of her face snapped Jade out of her trance. She blinked her eyes and looked at her daughter. "What?"

"I didn't think you were listening to me."

"I was, I promise."

One eyebrow arched, a trait Breanna had inherited from her father. "What did I just tell you?"

Biting her bottom lip, Jade gently shrugged.

"Here I go to the trouble to take you out to lunch on your birthday instead of studying for finals, and you aren't even paying any attention to me."

"I'm sorry, baby."

The teasing look disappeared from Breanna's eyes, to be replaced with concern. "Don't apologize to me, Mom. Something's obviously bothering you. Want to talk about it?"

Sharing her thoughts with her daughter had always helped Jade feel better. She took a sip of her drink to moisten her throat. "Two days ago, Zach and I went to Ridgmar Mall to see a movie. We got there early because I wanted to do a bit of shopping." She smiled slightly. "He was such a trooper, letting me take him from store to store when I'm sure he'd rather be buried beneath week-old fish than shop."

"He's a considerate guy."

"Yes, he is."

"So what's the problem?"

Jade picked up a French fry and swirled it in ketchup. "You know that area in the mall where the kids play?"

Breanna nodded.

"We were walking by it when we heard a woman call out 'Kevin' in a frantic voice. A crying toddler ran away from his mother and barreled right into Zach's legs." She laid the fry back in her plate without taking a bite of it. "He scooped Kevin up in his arms and thoroughly charmed him in only moments. By the time the woman had waded through everyone and got to us, the little guy was laughing and playing with Zach. In fact, he hesitated before he went back to his mother."

Breanna frowned. "I don't understand where you're going with this."

"Bre, Zach is a born father. He may not want children right now, but he will some day."

"Mom, you don't know that for sure."

"But what if he does? What if I stay involved with him and five years from now, he suddenly realizes what he's missing by not having children?"

"I think you're looking for trouble before it ever happens."

"I have to, Bre." Jade pushed her bangs off her forehead. "I've been with him for almost two weeks. Every moment has been incredible. He's the most wonderful man. Sexy, yes, but so much more than that. He makes me laugh. That's so important to me. I don't want to lose him."

"You won't." Breanna reached across the table and squeezed Jade's hand. "He loves you, Mom. I've seen the two of you together. The way he looks at you, with so much love and lust in his eyes, makes my heart hurt with jealousy."

Her joke made Jade chuckle. "Thanks, sweetie."

"He loves you as much as you love him. Don't throw that away because you're afraid of something that may never happen."

"In here," Jade touched her temple. "I know you're right. In here," she touched her chest over her heart. "I'm scared. Getting involved with a man ten years my junior was so stupid."

"You can't plan who you fall in love with, Mom."

"No, you can't, and that's precisely why I should've told him to leave my house first thing Sunday morning after the gala instead of continuing to see him."

Breanna sat back in her chair. "What are you going to do? Are you going to break up with him?"

"I should."

"No, you shouldn't. Mom, you *love* him. You've never been this happy in your life. I know you loved Dad, but he wasn't your soul mate. Zach is."

Breanna was right. Jade had never felt the depth of love for Carl that she felt for Zach. Despite knowing him only two weeks, she had no doubt about her feelings for him. It didn't seem possible that she could love him even more than she already did. She suspected as time passed, she'd only grow to love him more.

"Are you seeing Zach tonight?" Breanna asked.

"He's taking me out to dinner." Jade smiled, remembering the beautiful bouquet of two dozen red roses that had been delivered to her office this morning. "I told him my birth date the night of the gala. He remembered it. He sent me roses."

"Mom, you cannot give up a guy that romantic and loving."

Tears suddenly filled Jade's eyes. "I don't want to."

"Then don't." Breanna leaned forward again and rested her arms on the table. "Don't assume he'll want something in the future when you don't know for sure that'll happen." A hint of a grin turned up her lips. "Besides, I think having such a sexy stepfather will be cool."

Jade laughed. "You'll brag to all your girlfriends?"

"Damn right."

"I think you're rushing the stepfather bit."

"I don't. I wouldn't be a bit surprised if he proposed to you tonight."

"After only two weeks?"

Breanna shrugged. "Why wait when you know it's the real thing?"

* * * * *

Jade thought about her conversation with her daughter while she dressed for her date with Zach. She honestly didn't think he would propose marriage to her so soon. Two weeks was much too quick for something so serious.

She stood in her closet in the pale blue bra and panties she'd bought for herself today, trying to decide what to wear, when her doorbell rang. She knew it wouldn't be Breanna, and it was too early for Zach. Grabbing a robe, she quickly slipped it on while she walked down the hall.

She opened her front door, and gasped softly. Zach stood on her porch, looking like a model out of *GQ* in a navy suit, light gray shirt, and coordinating tie.

He smiled. "Good evening."

She returned his smile. "Good evening."

"I know I'm early, but I want to give you something before we leave for dinner."

Jade moved to the side. "Come in."

Zach stepped inside and she closed the door behind him. When she turned to face him, she saw him holding a single lilac rose.

Her heart swelled and a lump formed in her throat. "Another rose?" she said, her voice husky.

"A lilac rose means enchantment. That's what the florist told me. I thought that appropriate since I was completely enchanted the first time I saw you."

She accepted his rose, then his soft kiss. "Thank you," she whispered.

Cradling her cheek in his hand, he rubbed his thumb over her lips. "You're very welcome."

The love in his eyes stole her breath. She knew Carl had loved her, but he'd never looked at her with so much emotion, so much passion.

"Ready for your present?"

"The rose isn't my present?"

"Only an appetizer." Zach reached in his jacket pocket and drew out a small, rectangular box. "Happy birthday, Jade."

Her hands trembling, Jade reached for the black velvet box. She opened it, and gasped again when she saw the oval emerald surrounded by small diamonds. Tears sprang to her eyes. "Oh, Zach," she breathed.

"I wanted to get you something made of jade, but this necklace reminded me of the gown you wore on the night we met." He took the box from her hand. "May I put it on you?"

She nodded and turned her back to him. When she felt the cool stone against her chest, she lifted her hair so he could fasten the clasp. "You probably spent way too much money on this."

"So I'll buy cheaper carpet for the house." His lips touched her nape. "Turn around so I can see it."

Jade faced him again. He touched the stone and smiled. "Very nice." One finger dipped past the opening of her robe and into her cleavage. "I hope you have a dress that's low enough to show off the necklace and these beautiful breasts."

"I do."

His finger slipped inside her bra and over a nipple. "Need some help getting dressed?"

"That's not the way to help me get *dressed*."

He grinned wickedly. "Can I help it if I love your body?"

"You can love it all you want…later."

"Why not now?" He lightly pinched her nipple between his thumb and forefinger.

He didn't make it easy for her to be strong. "You'd have to take off your suit."

"Not to make you come." He tugged on the tie of her robe until her robe fell open, then slid his hand inside the front of her panties. "Mmm, you're getting wet already." He leaned forward and ran the tip of his tongue over her lips. "Let me make you come."

Summoning up all her willpower, she pulled his hands from her underwear. "Later, all right? I want us to make love together."

"I enjoy giving you pleasure, Jade."

"I know that." She squeezed his hands. "The feeling is mutual. But we have dinner reservations, and I don't want our lovemaking to be rushed."

"All right." He kissed her softly, then gave her a crooked grin. "I could still make you come."

She laughed. "Yes, you could. There's no doubt about that." She began walking down the hall, tugging him behind her. "You can pick out the dress I wear tonight."

* * * * *

Jade leaned against the doorframe and stared at the tiny sliver of moon. Tonight had been wonderful. A delicious dinner, a sinful dessert, dancing with the man she loved. She felt as she'd floated on a cloud all evening. And that was before she and Zach made love.

Every time he touched her, every time he slid his cock inside her, she loved him more.

She wiped a tear from her cheek. She should be lying in bed next to Zach. Instead, she stood at the patio door in her living room, alone in the dark, at one in the morning.

She loved Zach fiercely. She wanted to spend the rest of her life with him. But she didn't know how that could be possible.

Loving him meant putting his needs and desires above her own. No matter how much she loved Zach, she had to think about him and his future. She had to do what was best for him.

That meant she had to end their relationship.

He'd find someone else…someone closer to his age, someone who could give him children. A man so good with kids would want his own. Perhaps children weren't important to him now, but they would be someday. She had no doubt about that.

To give him happiness, she had to give up her own. She loved him enough to do that.

She started when she felt Zach's hands on her waist.

"What's wrong, babe?" He kissed the side of her neck. "Can't you sleep?"

How can I do this? How can I break up with him without falling apart?

She quickly wiped the tears from her eyes before he saw them. "I've...been thinking."

"About what?"

"About us."

His arms slid around her waist. "I like the sound of that."

"No, I don't think you will." Her heart pounded in her chest. Swallowing hard for courage, she turned to face him. "This isn't working, Zach."

"What isn't working?"

"You and me."

He took a step backward. "What?"

"I said I'd give us a chance and I did, but it isn't working."

He moved away from her. A moment later, he turned on a lamp. Jade blinked at the sudden light. "What do you mean, it isn't working?"

His eyebrows drew together and he frowned. His confusion didn't surprise Jade. She'd given him no indication that something could be wrong between them. "I can't... I can't get past our age difference, Zach. Ten years is too much."

He shoved his hair off his forehead and huffed out a breath. "Jade, we've been over this a dozen times. I love you. I don't care that you're older than me. It doesn't matter."

"It doesn't matter now, but what about in the future? What happens when I get wrinkles and gray hair?"

"What happens if I gain fifty pounds? Will you stop loving me if I no longer look like a stud?"

"Of course not. Love isn't based on physical looks."

"Then why do you insist on worrying about something that may never happen?"

"I *have* to, Zach. I have to think with my head and not my heart." Her voice broke on the last word. Jade blinked back tears that rushed to her eyes again. She couldn't weaken now.

"We made love a few hours ago," Zach said, pointing toward the bedroom. "We *made love,* Jade. It wasn't sex. Our souls, our hearts, connected as well as our bodies. How can you give that up?"

"A relationship has to be more than sex, Zach."

"*Shit*!" He turned, took two steps away from her, then faced her again. The blazing anger in his eyes made her take a step back and cross her arms over her stomach. "We have a lot more than sex, Jade, you know that. I can get sex from any woman."

She pointedly looked at his naked cock. "I'm well aware of that."

His eyes narrowed. "Is that a dig about my former job?"

"No, it isn't a dig. I know you've had sex with a lot of women. What happened in the past doesn't matter."

"Neither should our ages." He walked up to her and clasped her upper arms. She now saw anguish mixed with anger. How she hated hurting him. "You wouldn't do this if our ages were reversed, if I were ten years older than you."

"That's different."

"Why? Because it's 'socially acceptable' for the man to be older, but not the woman? I don't give a damn about what's socially acceptable or not. I only care about being with you."

"I can't have any more children, Zach."

"I don't care! I've already told you that."

She opened her mouth to argue further, but he spoke again before she could utter a word. "And don't give me any bullshit about me wanting children down the road. Maybe I will, maybe I won't. And maybe I'll get hit by a truck on my way to the grocery store. I won't let the fear of that possibility keep me from driving." He squeezed her arms. "I want a life with you, Jade. *You*. I love you."

Tears filled her eyes and overflowed. "I can't, Zach," she whispered. "I just can't."

He released her and stepped back. "So this is it. You're throwing away what we have because of fear."

"Yes," she rasped.

He stared at her another moment, then turned and walked down the hall.

Jade covered her mouth to stifle her sobs. Her knees buckled. She locked them to keep from falling to the floor. She had to do this. No matter how much it hurt her and Zach now, she had to do this. He would find someone else to love, someone who would make him happy.

He came back in the living room, now dressed. He strode directly up to her, grabbed her neck, and kissed her savagely.

Surprised at his action, Jade stop breathing. When his tongue dove past her lips, she inhaled sharply and moaned.

God, she loved him.

The kiss ended as quickly as it had started. "I'm so angry at you for doing this. I'm angry that you aren't strong enough to fight for something so good. But I'm not giving up on us. I'll give you time to think about what you're doing. When you decide you're ready to spend your life with me, come to me. I'll be waiting."

He walked out the front door…and out of her life.

Chapter Eighteen

ꟷ

The headache pounded behind Jade's eyes. Sitting across the wide oak table from Doug Lassiter wasn't helping her pain to lessen.

She could feel him watching her. Refusing to play his perverted game, she concentrated on the Chairman of the Board's words. Everything he said began to run together. She felt as if there wasn't enough oxygen in the air.

If she didn't get out of this room soon, she feared she might faint. Or scream.

Ten minutes later, the chairman called a halt to the meeting. Silently breathing a sigh of relief, Jade began to gather up her paperwork, intending to make a fast getaway.

"Jade, I need to speak with you…in private."

He'd finally cornered her. She'd avoided him for almost four weeks, thinking he'd give up on his silly blackmail threat. Apparently, he didn't give up easily…along with several other men who worked in the hospital. Jade had never fended off so many interested suitors in her life. If she accepted dates from every man who asked her out, she'd be booked every night for the next month.

A daring dress and a younger man had certainly perked up everyone's opinion of her sexuality. She didn't know whether to be flattered or angry.

It was time to put an end to this. She turned to face Doug. "I don't have much time, Dr. Lassiter."

"This won't take much time. We can talk in my office."

There was no way she'd be alone in an elevator with him, even in the hospital. "I need to take care of a couple of things first. I can be in your office in fifteen minutes."

A hint of a frown drew his eyebrows together, but he nodded. "Fine. Fifteen minutes."

Jade took her time getting the rest of her paperwork together. If Doug Lassiter had to wait a few minutes for her, fine. He'd soon learn he couldn't blackmail her into *anything*.

It didn't surprise her to find his office door closed. She knocked once, then turned the doorknob and stepped inside without waiting for him to bid her to enter.

He sat behind his massive cherry-wood desk. The hospital's administrator didn't even have a desk that huge. The man was so full of himself, Jade was surprised his head didn't explode from his oversized ego. "You wanted to talk to me?" she asked.

"Close the door, Jade."

"I'd rather leave it open."

"As you wish, but I wouldn't think you'd want anyone who happened to walk by knowing your business."

He had a point there, damn him. Jade shut the door and leaned against it. "I don't have much time, Doug."

"Then I'll get right to the point." He stood, rounded his desk, and leaned against it, ankles crossed. "I've given you four weeks to think about my...proposal. That's plenty of time."

"You're right. That's plenty of time. I don't need a second longer to tell you to stuff your proposal right up..." She stopped and smiled sweetly. "Well, you get the idea."

Doug made a "tsking" sound. It grated on Jade's nerves and made her long to slap the smug look off his face.

"Now, Jade, you know I hold all the cards. Why don't you just give in gracefully?"

Slowly, she strolled toward him. "It's been a month since the gala. I just spent two hours in a meeting with every member of the board. Not one of them has said a word to me about my dress, my date, or possibly losing my job. In fact, Dr. Jennings praised my work today, saying he's totally satisfied with my performance." She stopped in front of him. "Now, why do you suppose he would say something like that if the board meant to fire me?"

His cocky smile slipped a little. Jade fought to keep from grinning in triumph. "Cat got your tongue, doctor?"

"I-I can still destroy you—"

"Oh, save it for someone who might believe you. I know your reputation, Doug. You'll have sex with any woman who raises her skirt. I don't know why Marianne puts up with it, but she does because I don't believe for one moment that she doesn't know about all your affairs." She rammed her finger into the middle of his chest. "Well, you know what, Dr. Lassiter? I'm not that desperate for sex, nor will I *ever* be that desperate for sex."

His lips thinned into a hard line. "No, not with your young stud fucking you."

Jade almost flinched, but caught herself before he had the chance to see how much his words hurt her. "The age of my stud is none of your business, nor the business of anyone else in this hospital. I keep my personal and business lives totally separate."

She turned and hurried to the door. With her hand on the knob, she looked at him again. "I'm a professional at this hospital, Dr. Lassiter. It's too bad you can't say the same thing."

Head held high, Jade left his office and headed for the stairs. She needed the brisk walk up two flights of steps right now to cool off.

Zach would've been so proud of her.

She wouldn't allow any tears to fall. Once inside her office with the door closed, she closed her eyes tightly and bit her bottom lip to keep from crying.

She missed him so much. This last week without him had been the hardest week of her life. The pain had almost destroyed her when Carl walked out of her life. That pain was a ride on a Ferris wheel compared to this.

Being strong really sucked.

The ringing of her cell phone dragged her away from the door. Picking it up from her desk, she peeked at the display to see Breanna's phone number. She swallowed hard before she flipped open the phone.

"Hi, honey."

"Hi. You busy?"

"I just got out of the board meeting."

"Borrrrring."

"Yes, but a necessity." She sat down in her chair and pushed her hair back from her face. "What's up?"

"You wanna hang out with your daughter tonight? Go out to eat, see a movie, stuff like that?"

"What? You don't have a date?"

"Mom, it's Monday."

"There's a rule you don't date on Monday?"

Jade smiled when she heard Breanna sigh. "Mommmm!"

"Sorry."

"Do you want to go out or not?"

"Sounds great. When and where?"

"Let's try that new Chinese place in Burleson. I've heard it's—"

"Burleson? Honey, that's miles from where you..." She stopped when she realized what her daughter was doing. "No."

"I think you should show me Zach's house. You said it's gorgeous. I want to see it."

"No."

"Maybe he'll be there, working on it."

"*No.*"

"Then you can talk to him."

"*NO.*"

"Mom, you can't leave it this way. You're miserable without him."

"Breanna, whether or not I'm miserable isn't the issue. I want what's best for Zach."

"He loves you. *You're* what's best for him."

"Oh, honey." Jade leaned her head back on her chair and rubbed her forehead. Her headache began to pound again. "You're still so young and have so much to learn about life. Sometimes you have to make sacrifices for the ones you love."

"I understand that, Mom, I do. But this isn't what you want, and it sure as hell isn't what Zach wants. And *don't* tell me to watch my language. I'm mad. I cuss when I'm mad."

Jade couldn't help chuckling. "Yes, I know."

"Please, Mom? Will you talk to him?"

"No, Bre, I won't."

"I can't believe you're so stubborn!"

"I'm doing what's right. Zach..." Her voice cracked on his name. She had to swallow before she could continue. "Zach will find someone else to love, someone closer to his age."

"You know what? If you weren't my mother, I'd slug you."

"I love you, too, Bre."

Breanna sighed heavily. "Will you still go to a movie with me, if I promise not to bug you about Zach?"

An evening with her daughter would take her mind off the man she loved…at least for a while. "I'd like that."

* * * * *

"You okay with this, Zach?" Brent asked.

"Yeah. Whatever."

Zach stared out the window at his sister. She'd been excited earlier because she'd found some kind of flowers on sale. Now she was outside, happily planting them in the flowerbeds.

"So you agree we should let Michelle dance naked in the yard to entice new escorts, right?"

"Yeah. Sure."

"With flowers hanging from her nipples."

"Sounds good."

"Zach. Zach. ZACHARY!"

Hearing his name shouted finally sunk into Zach's head. He turned and looked at his brother. "What!"

Brent scowled. "Well, *finally* I have your attention. Where the hell are you today?" His scowl deepened. "Or should I even ask that?"

"Don't bug me today, Brent. I'm not in the mood."

"Apparently. You haven't been in a mood for anything lately, especially business."

Zach looked out the window again. "You don't need me for the business. You and Michelle can run it without me."

"You're an equal partner, Zach. We need your signature on the dotted line, too."

After one more look at his sister, he wandered over to Brent's desk and flopped down in a chair. "Put whatever you need in front of me. I'll sign."

"Jesus, you're pathetic."

His uncaring attitude made Zach's anger flare. "Well, excuse me if I don't feel like turning cartwheels."

"If that's what love does to you, I want no part of it."

Zach pushed his hair back from his forehead. He rested his head on the chair and stared at the ceiling. He didn't care if he ate or slept. He worked every moment he could on his house, until exhaustion drove him to bed. Only then could he sleep without dreaming of Jade.

He never would have believed love could hurt so much.

"You need something to get your mind off…her."

"I'm working on my house."

"That isn't enough. You need to go out, have a good time, get laid."

Zach lowered his head and glared at his brother. "Brent—"

"Take out one of these ladies," Brent said, holding up several sheets of paper. "They're clamoring for you, man. Dipping your dick into a honeypot will put the smile back on your face."

"Aw, *shit*!" Zach stood up so quickly, the chair fell over and crashed to the floor. "I don't believe you. I don't fuckin' believe you! You're twenty-eight years old. When the hell are you gonna grow up? Sex with some nameless woman isn't going to put a smile on my face! I love Jade. I know you can't understand that concept, but I don't want to be with any other woman."

Frowning, Brent also stood and leaned on the desk. "No, I don't understand that concept. I'm sorry you're hurting, but—"

"You aren't sorry." He gestured toward the papers on Brent's desk. "All you care about is making more money. I'm Coopers' Companions' highest paid escort. A nice percentage of what I bring in goes right into your pocket."

"I've never seen you turn down a paycheck, big brother, especially since you started building your fancy house."

Zach stared at his brother. There were other things he wanted to say…hurtful things. He had to get out of here before he said or did something to drive a further wedge between them.

"I'm outta here," he muttered.

Once outside the house, Zach took a deep breath of the warm spring air, hoping it would calm him. He didn't like arguing with his brother. He was just so damn *angry*.

He was angry at Brent, at himself, and especially at Jade for hurting him.

He needed to do something physical. He needed to pound nails, use a power saw, haul two-by-fours. The work at his house had kept him sane the last week. Working up a good sweat would be great for getting rid of his frustration.

Michelle looked up from the flowerbed as he walked toward her. "You leaving?"

"Yeah. I'm going out to the house."

She sat back on her haunches and shielded the sun from her eyes with her hand. "Did you and Brent fight again?"

"We can't seem to do anything lately but fight."

"He loves you, Zach. You know that."

"Yeah, I know that, and I love him, but he..." Not wanting to say anything negative to his sister, Zach stopped. "We disagree on some things."

"He wants you to be an escort again."

"That's one of the things we disagree on."

"Do you think you'll ever change your mind?"

He sighed. "I don't know, Chelle. Maybe someday, but no time soon. I'm just... I can't think about being with another woman now."

"You could escort some of our regular clients, the ladies who don't want sex."

"I wouldn't be very good company for them."

She stood, wrapped her arms around his neck, and hugged him tightly. Zach returned her hug, then simply held her for several moments, absorbing her love and caring.

"Do you need some help at your house?"

Zach clasped her hands and squeezed them. "Sure. How are you at painting?"

She grinned. "Almost as good as gardening."

"Sold."

"I'll come out this afternoon." She tilted her head and bit her bottom lip. "Do you want me to bring Brent?"

"I could use his muscle with the sheetrock, but I don't want to argue with him anymore about escorting."

"Don't worry. I'll make sure he knows talking about anything to do with Coopers' Companions is *not* allowed."

Chapter Nineteen

ഗ

Jade plucked a weed hiding beneath a patch of red pansies. The beautiful spring day had beckoned to her, calling her out of her house into the sunshine. She'd done little more than go to work and hibernate inside the house for the last two weeks…ever since Zach walked out of her life.

Thinking of him sent a stabbing pain through her heart. She'd lost seven pounds because food held no appeal to her. Her eyes burned from lack of sleep. She hadn't allowed herself to cry. Once she started crying, she was afraid she'd never stop.

Not even her divorce from Carl had caused her this much agony.

Every day, she told herself she should go to Zach. Every day, she told herself she couldn't. For him to be happy later, she had to hurt him now. Her own pain didn't matter. She only wanted Zach to be happy.

She looked up when she heard a vehicle pull into her driveway. She didn't recognize it. Pulling off her gloves, she stood and waited for the driver to get out of the vehicle.

She was shocked to see her ex-husband climb down from the SUV.

"Carl?"

"Hi, Jade."

He walked toward her. Jade let her gaze quickly travel over him. He wore a pair of faded jeans and a short-sleeved polo shirt. Strands of gray liberally streaked his dark brown hair. She hadn't seen him since their divorce hearing. Always a good-looking man, he'd retained those good looks as he'd grown older.

"What are you doing here?"

"I'd like to talk to you." He gave her a small smile. "Can we go inside, maybe have a glass of tea?"

Carl hadn't come to see her in two years. She had no idea why he would be here, unless he needed to talk to her about their daughter. "Uh, sure. Of course. Is this about Breanna?"

"No."

He didn't elaborate. Jade glanced at him over her shoulder as she led the way to the kitchen. "Then why are you here?"

"Let's talk while we drink our tea, all right?"

She motioned toward the kitchen table. "Sit down and I'll get the tea."

Jade glanced at Carl often while she washed her hands and prepared their drinks. He fidgeted. Carl had never fidgeted. He was a strong man who knew exactly what he wanted. Right now, with his eyes darting around the room and his feet shuffling beneath the table, he didn't look strong. He looked nervous.

She joined him at the table, setting their glasses down before taking the chair opposite him. "What's going on, Carl? Why are you here?"

He took a gulp of his tea before he spoke. "I guess you see Bre pretty often, huh?"

"I talk to her every day and see her two to three times a week."

"Did she tell you about…Melody?"

"She told me y'all broke up."

"Yeah." He huffed out a breath and sat back in his chair. "I screwed up, Jade."

Now his fidgeting made sense. He regretted his breakup with Melody. She reached across the table and touched his hand. "Talk to her, Carl. Maybe you can work things out."

"I didn't screw things up with Melody. I screwed them up with you."

Jade snatched back her hand as if his skin were burning hot. "What?"

"I never should have left you. You were the best thing that ever happened to me."

She had absolutely no idea what to say to his declaration.

Carl leaned forward again and rested his arms on the table. "You aren't involved with anyone, are you, Jade? Is there any way you'd give me another chance?"

"You aren't serious."

"Yes, I am. I didn't realize how good I had it with you until I lost you."

"You didn't lose me, Carl. You left me."

His gaze lowered to the table a moment before he looked at her again. "I regret that, Jade. I can't tell you how much I regret that. I want another chance to make everything right with you. I've missed you."

"Oh, Carl." Reaching across the table again, she took both his hands in hers. "I love you. I'll always love you. You were my first lover, my husband. You're Breanna's father. But I'm not in love with you."

A tiny flare of hope flashed through his eyes. "Maybe you could fall in love with me again?"

Sympathy swelled in her heart. He looked like a lost little boy instead of the domineering man she knew him to be. Jade shook her head. "No. I'm sorry. I don't... I can't feel that way about you again, Carl. I'm in love with someone else."

The hope died in his eyes. "Oh." He lifted her hands to his mouth and kissed the back of both. "I thought it was worth a try."

She blinked away the tears in her eyes at his tender action. "I really am sorry."

"Yeah. Me too." He released her hands. "You really love him?"

"I really do."

"Then I guess I'd better get out of here."

"You're always welcome in my home, Carl."

He smiled sadly. "Thanks, Jade."

She walked him to the door. He opened it, then looked back at her. Cradling her face in one hand, he lightly caressed her cheek.

"You're lucky to find love again, Jade. Don't ever let it go, no matter what. I did, and I'll regret it for the rest of my life."

Her throat tightened when he kissed her softly, making speech impossible. She closed the door behind him and leaned her forehead against the wood. Her throat began to burn. Tears flooded her eyes. A sob tore from her mouth.

"Zach," she whispered.

Jade's legs buckled and she slid to the floor. Covering her face with her hands, she shed the tears she'd been holding back for two weeks. Sobs racked her body. She wrapped her arms across her churning stomach as the tears flowed down her cheeks. She'd pushed away the man she loved because she'd been afraid of losing him, afraid he'd want more than she could give him.

She missed him so much.

I'm not giving up on us. I'll give you time to think about what you're doing. When you decide you're ready to spend your life with me, come to me. I'll be waiting.

Zach's final words echoed inside her head. Jade drew her knees up to her chest, propped her elbows on them, and pressed the heels of her hands into her stinging eyes. She had been stupid—incredibly stupid. There were no guarantees in life. A relationship took effort to make it work. All couples had problems. But with patience, understanding, and a lot of love, those problems could be worked out.

She and Zach definitely had a lot of love.

Did you mean it, Zach? Will you take me back if I go to you, if I tell you how sorry I am to have let you go?

She had to try, right now, this moment. He might throw her out on her butt, but she had to try. She didn't want to live one more hour without him.

Pushing herself up from the floor, she headed down the hall toward her bedroom. As soon as she showered and dressed, she was going to find the man she loved.

* * * * *

"How's it look?" Michelle asked.

Zach wiped a smudge of pale blue paint from his sister's nose. "Like you're getting more paint on you than on the wall."

Michelle swiped her brush at him. Zach quickly darted to the side to avoid getting a blue chest.

"I could be lying by a pool somewhere with a gorgeous hunk. Instead, I'm helping my brother paint his house. You should consider yourself lucky to be getting all this free labor."

"Hear, hear," Brent said with a grin. He walked into the guest room carrying three bottles of beer. "You've definitely taken advantage of us these last few days, bro."

"I want to get the house finished."

Michelle accepted a beer from Brent. "Working yourself to death won't make you forget her, Zach."

Zach froze with the beer bottle halfway to his mouth. His gaze darted to his sister. "Forget who?"

She scowled at him. "Don't act stupid. We know you're hurting. We just don't want you to do anything you'll regret."

Swallowing his mouthful of beer, Zach wiped off his lips with the back of his hand. "If you're worried I'm gonna put a gun to my head, you can relax. Life's too short to consider suicide."

"There are other ways to hurt yourself. You've lived in this house the last two weeks, working almost nonstop. You sleep on a pallet, when you sleep at all. I'll bet you don't get more than three or four hours a night."

"If I'm lucky," he muttered.

"Zach—

"I'm fine, Chelle. No one dies of a broken heart."

"No, but they can hurt like hell," Brent said.

Zach faced his brother. "You were the one who didn't want me to get involved with Jade."

"Yeah, well, I was being selfish. You know I do that very well." He clapped Zach on the shoulder. "I want you to be happy, bro. That's the most important thing."

The support of his siblings meant the world to Zach. They'd been by his side at every possible moment the last two weeks as he tried to put his heart back together. "Thanks, man," he said, his voice husky.

Michelle's eyes glistened with tears. If she started crying, he'd lose it. "Okay, break over. Back to work."

She blinked away her tears and frowned playfully. "Can't I even finish my beer?"

"You can drink and paint at the same time."

"Slave driver."

Zach grinned and kissed her cheek. "Yeah, but you love me."

He turned to leave the room, but stopped when he thought he heard a noise outside. He looked back at his brother. "Was that a car?"

"It sounded like it."

"Who'd come out here to the boonies?" Michelle asked.

"It might be the carpet people," Brent said. "I'll check it out."

* * * * *

Jade climbed from her car. She smoothed her damp palms down her denim skirt and checked to be sure her T-shirt was tucked into the waistband. She'd taken a chance that Zach would be here, working on his house. She didn't see his car, nor did she recognize the two pickups parked beneath the huge oak tree.

"Well, you definitely aren't the carpet guys."

She looked back at the house when she heard the male voice. A handsome blond man stood on the porch, wearing a pair of denim cutoffs. He didn't look happy to see her. "No, I'm not the carpet guys."

His gaze slowly passed over her. Jade had the feeling she'd just been inspected. "You must be Jade."

He knew her? "Yes, I am." She cleared her throat. "Is Zach here?"

The blond pointed over his shoulder with his thumb. "He's inside."

She took three steps toward the porch. He didn't move from his spot in front of the door. "Are you the guard?"

"If I need to be to keep you from hurting my brother again."

His brother. Then this must be Brent. She could think of a dozen better ways to meet the man who she hoped would be her future brother-in-law. "The last thing I want to do is hurt your brother."

His scowl indicated he didn't believe her. She stood still, waiting for him to move. It was obvious he didn't trust her, but she would not leave until she spoke with Zach. If he threw her out, so be it. She at least had to try to convince him to forgive her.

Brent stared at her another moment, then turned and walked inside the house. "This way," he called over his shoulder.

Jade followed Brent into the house. She looked around her, admiring all the work Zach had done. The house was beautiful…spacious, airy, light. The carpet hadn't been laid yet, but the rooms she walked by were complete. A peek into the kitchen as she passed it made her gasp in pleasure.

He glanced at her. "You okay?"

"Yes. The house is gorgeous."

"Zach's a talented carpenter."

She could hear muted conversation and The Eagles' "Take It to the Limit" as they walked down the hall. The sound of Zach's deep voice made her stomach do flip-flops.

Brent led her into what she remembered as being one of the guest rooms. "Zach, Jade is here."

He turned to face her. Jade stopped breathing. The sight of him sweaty, dressed in nothing but a pair of denim cutoffs like his brother, caused her heart to skitter in her chest.

The anger in his eyes made her cringe.

"Hey, Michelle," Brent said, "I'm getting hungry. How about if we go pick up some pizzas?"

The lovely brunette standing next to Zach frowned. Her gaze traveled between Jade and Zach, as if she were considering whether or not to leave her brother unprotected.

"C'mon, Chelle. They need to talk."

Michelle looked at Zach again. He nodded.

If looks could kill, Michelle's glare would have turned Jade into a pile of ashes. Both she and Brent obviously loved their brother very much.

Jade silently stared at Zach until she heard doors slam and the start of a pickup's engine. The noise jarred her into taking a step toward him. Not sure what to say, she said a simple, "Hi."

"Hi."

Well, that didn't work. "Your house is beautiful, Zach. You've done so much work on it in a month."

"Brent and Michelle have helped a lot." He set the bottle of beer he'd been holding on a windowsill. "I doubt you came here to talk about my house, Jade. Why *are* you here?"

Jade clasped her hands together to stop their trembling. "I had a visitor today."

His eyebrows arched, but he said nothing.

"Carl came to see me."

"Your ex-husband?"

"Yes. He asked me if I'd be willing to give him another chance."

Pain darted through his eyes before he looked away from her. His reaction gave her hope. He wouldn't hurt if he didn't still care for her. Jade took another step closer. "I told him no."

Zach looked back at her. "Why?"

"Because I'm not in love with him. I'm in love with you."

A pulse beat in his temple. "Then why did you break up with me?"

Three more steps brought her close enough to touch him. She laid one hand in the middle of his chest. His heart pounded beneath her palm. "I was scared, Zach—scared of how quickly I fell in love with you, scared you'd decide you'd made a mistake in becoming involved with an older woman, scared you'd want the children I can't give you." She touched his mouth with her fingertips. "Carl told me I'm lucky to find love again and shouldn't ever let it go. He was right." Tears flooded her eyes. "You told me you'd wait for me. Did you mean that, or am I too late? Do you love me enough to give me another chance? Do you love me enough to forgive me for hurting you?"

His eyes narrowed. A muscle jumped in his jaw. "So if your ex-husband hadn't come to see you today, you wouldn't be here."

Jade started to disagree with his statement, but she honestly couldn't. "I don't know."

He moved back from her. "I think you'd better go."

The possibility that he wouldn't forgive her made her stomach tighten into a knot. "Wait. Please hear me out."

"There's nothing for me to hear, Jade. You just admitted Carl's visit made you come here. So if your ex-husband hadn't suddenly decided he wanted you back, you never would have come to me. I wish you hadn't. Seeing you makes me angry all over again." Turning away from her, he gestured toward the door. "Get out of here. I have work to do."

Jade swiped at the tears on her cheeks. "Zach, please listen to me. I don't know if I would've come to you *today*, but I would have come. I've been so miserable without you. A day, an hour, hasn't gone by that I haven't thought of you." She stepped close to him again. "Carl's visit made me realize how much I need you. Don't turn me away. Please."

He whirled around to face her. "That's exactly what you did to me, Jade. I gave you my love, my soul, and you turned me away. Now I'm supposed to simply forget the way you trampled on my heart and forgive you?"

"I'm sorry." Her voice cracked. "I never meant to hurt you."

"But you did, Jade. I'm having a hard time getting over that."

The agony in his eyes clutched at her heart. She didn't know what to do to make things better between them.

More tears filled her eyes and her nose began to run. "I need a tissue please."

He stuffed his hands in the pockets of his shorts. "The bathroom's across the hall."

Jade left the room and crossed the hall. She could barely see, her tears were falling so quickly. Rolling off a long piece of toilet paper, she blew her nose. She'd made such a horrible mistake in breaking up with Zach. She'd thrown away the love of a wonderful man in fear of something that might never happen.

She didn't know what to do to get him back.

She dropped the soiled paper in the wastebasket and turned. Zach stood in the doorway, watching her.

Chapter Twenty

ஐ

Zach leaned against the bathroom doorway and studied Jade. Her nose was red, her eyes puffy. She'd obviously been crying for a long time.

Despite his anger, his heart swelled with sympathy and love.

"Better?" he asked.

"Yes. Thank you."

"Would you like a drink of water?"

"No. I'm…" She stopped and tears filled her eyes again. "I can't do this. I can't stand here and have this asinine conversation with you!"

Zach sighed heavily. "What do you want from me, Jade?"

"I want you to love me again."

"I never stopped loving you. I'll love you until the day I die."

"Then why won't you forgive me? I made a mistake, Zach, and I'm sorry. But I thought I was doing what was best for you."

"I know," he said softly.

And he did know that. Jade was a thoughtful, caring person who put the needs of others before her own. Breaking up with him had been because she loved him.

She wiped the wetness from her cheeks. "Do you still want me to go?"

He wanted to take her in his arms and never let go. He shook his head. "No, I don't want you to go."

She took one step closer to him. "Does that mean you'll give me another chance?"

"Are you sure, Jade? You have to tell me you're sure, because I can't—I *won't*—go through this pain again."

"I am absolutely sure. I swear I'll never hurt you again. I love you." She walked up to him, wrapped her arms around his neck, and hugged him tightly. "*I love you,*" she said, her voice breaking.

For the first time in two weeks, Zach could breathe without the sharp pain in his chest. Wrapping his arms around Jade, he returned her fierce hug. He stood with her in his embrace, her tears dampening his shoulder, while he fought his own battle with tears.

He loved her more than his own life.

Several moments passed before he sought her lips with his. He kissed her slowly, tenderly, with all the love in his heart. His body responded to her nearness, his shaft growing longer, thicker. He tried to ignore his randy cock. The feel of Jade's soft breasts pressed against his chest made that impossible.

She kissed his chin, his cheek, his jaw. "How long will Michelle and Brent be gone?"

Zach swallowed when her tongue darted into his ear. "At least an hour."

"Make love to me, Zach."

"I don't have a bed yet. I've been sleeping on a pallet."

"I don't need a bed. I just need you."

"I've been working all day. I'm pretty sweaty."

She frowned. "You certainly have a lot of excuses. Do you want me naked or not?"

Zach chuckled. "Well, when you put it that way..."

Taking her hand, he led her down the hall to his bedroom. He'd placed the pallet beneath the south windows so he could take advantage of the pleasant night air while he fell asleep. It was also hidden from view of the door opening, in case Michelle and Brent came back before he expected them to.

Kneeling on the pallet, he tugged on Jade's hand until she knelt before him. He quickly pulled off her T-shirt and removed her bra, needing to feel her bare flesh as soon as possible. Once she was naked from the waist up, he drew her back into his arms. Her breasts felt full and warm against his chest.

How easy it would be to take her fast. The two weeks without her seemed more like two months. He knew if he entered her now, he'd come much too soon. He had to push aside his own needs to take care of her first. "Lie down, Jade."

Jade lay on her back, her head resting on his pillow. "Lift your hips." She did, and he pulled off her skirt, panties, and sandals with one jerk. Pushing her thighs apart, he lowered his mouth to her pussy.

She was already wet and swollen. Zach inhaled deeply of the scent he loved before he touched her clit with the tip of his tongue. Jade buried her hands in his hair and held his head close to her. He licked her folds slow and gentle, the way he knew built up her desire to a feverish pitch.

"Zach, I need you—Oh, *God*, that feels good!—inside me."

He nipped her thigh. "Not yet, babe. Not until you come." Spreading her lips with his thumbs, he speared his tongue into her slit. "Mmm, you taste so good."

She arched her back and pulled his hair. He didn't care. She could pull out every hair on his head as long as she came.

Zach wet his thumb with her juices and circled her anus. Jade spread her legs another inch. He concentrated on her clit—licking, sucking, nipping—as he worked his thumb inside her ass.

A keening moan signaled the start of her climax. She bucked her hips as he pushed his thumb all the way into her ass and suckled her clit.

"Zach!"

Her anus contracted around his thumb. He continued to softly lick her folds as her body relaxed. When she finally released the death grip on his hair, he rose to his knees and unfastened his cutoffs.

"Turn over, babe."

Zach didn't take the time to remove his shorts. He couldn't wait any longer to be inside her. Slipping one arm beneath her stomach, he lifted her and drove his shaft into her pussy with one thrust.

Tight, wet heat. Zach almost came as soon as he entered her. He took a breath and rested his forehead on Jade's shoulder, trying to bring his hormones back under control. He didn't want to come yet. It was too soon.

Jade gripped his thigh with one hand. "Zach, please," she rasped, raising her hips.

"Give me a second, sweetheart. I don't want to be rough with you."

"I don't care if you're rough. Take me however you need to."

Her words made him groan. Later, he and Jade would make love with soft music and candlelight. Now, he needed to fuck her slick pussy rough and fast.

He began to pump his hips, driving his cock deep inside her. "Raise your ass more. Yeah, like that."

Her whimper urged him to thrust even faster. Soon he was gripping her waist and pounding his shaft into her pussy so hard, he pushed her up on the pallet. Jade braced her hands against the wall, rose to her knees, and spread her legs farther.

Raw. Earthy. Incredibly hot. All those words came to Zach's mind to describe their fucking. His orgasm built in the base of his spine and grabbed his balls. He fought it, trying to draw it out as long as possible. He wanted Jade to come again before he did.

He licked his thumb and pushed it into her ass.

The walls of her pussy milked his shaft. The sensation urged him toward his own release. Zach groaned loudly as his climax tightened his balls. With a final lunge into her wet heat, he came deep inside her.

Despite a powerful orgasm, his cock remained hard. Withdrawing his shaft from her body, he rolled Jade to her back. Holding both her wrists over her head, he surged into her again.

Her eyes were wide and tear-filled, making them sparkle like emeralds. He knew her tears this time weren't from sorrow, but from the powerful sensations in her body.

Zach stared into her eyes as he drove his penis into her over and over. Tears slowly fell from the corners of her eyes into her hair. He licked each tear away from her temples, then covered her mouth with his. Parting his lips, he accepted the play of her tongue. He bit it lightly, then sucked it farther into his mouth.

Jade responded with a loud moan. She arched her back and wrapped her legs around his hips. Zach released one of her wrists and slipped his hand beneath her buttocks. He lifted her higher to him so he could thrust even deeper.

He trailed kisses up her neck to her ear. "I love you, Jade," he whispered.

"I love you, too. So very much."

"Come for me, sweetheart. I need to feel you come again."

He'd barely said the words when her body began to shudder from her third orgasm. Zach's own climax raced through his body. Holding her tightly, he rode the wave with her.

Since he knew his tongue wouldn't work yet, he didn't even try to talk for several moments. When Jade unwrapped her legs from around his waist, he drew enough strength to raise his head.

"Wow."

She giggled. "I'll go along with that."

He kissed the tip of her nose. "You are incredible in bed, lady."

She slid her hands down to his buttocks and lightly scratched them. "I have an amazing partner."

"We're really good together."

"Yes, we are."

He reluctantly withdrew from her body. Moving to his back, he pulled her into his arms. Jade wrapped one arm around his waist and rested her head on his shoulder. Content to simply hold her, he remained silent while slowly stroking her back.

"Your house is beautiful, Zach. You're a very talented carpenter."

"I like working with my hands."

She tilted back her head and grinned at him. "I know."

He playfully scowled at her. "Sex, sex, sex. That's all you think about."

"And you're complaining?"

"What, you think I'm crazy? I love that you want me as much as you do."

Her fingers combed through his chest hair. "You make it easy to want you."

Cradling her jaw in his hand, Zach tilted up her face and kissed her. "Move in here with me, Jade."

Her eyes widened. "What?"

"Move in with me. Help me finish decorating this house the way you want it done. Michelle picked out the paint colors, but they can be changed if you don't like them."

"Everything is perfect. Michelle did a wonderful job."

"I haven't picked out curtains or carpet yet, and it's obvious I don't have any furniture. The carpet guys are supposed to be here this afternoon to measure. I think they'll have samples with them you could look at."

"Zach, are you sure? We've only known each other five weeks."

"Living together will give us the chance to find out more about each other. There's still a lot about you I don't know. For instance, I don't even know if you like beer."

She snorted with laughter. "Actually, no, I don't."

"That's it. The relationship is over. I can't be involved with a woman who doesn't like beer."

"I like sex. Does that count?"

Grinning, he dipped his hand down to her buttock and squeezed. "Oh, yeah. That counts big time."

Turning serious again, he gave her another soft kiss. "Live with me, Jade. Be my lover, my wife."

"The mother of your children?"

Startled at her question, he didn't respond for a moment. "What?"

"I've...thought about it. If you ever do decide you want to be a father, maybe we could adopt, or hire a surrogate mother, or...something."

"You said you'd be happy to wait for grandchildren."

"That was before I fell in love with you. Besides," she said with a twinkle in her eyes, "the way Bre goes through men, I doubt I'll be a grandmother any time soon."

The thought that Jade would do something so unselfish for him made his throat tighten. It was no wonder he loved this woman so much.

"I want you to be happy, Zach."

"I want *both* of us to be happy."

"As long as I'm with you, I will be."

"Does that mean you'll move in here with me?"

She nodded. "Yes, I'll move in here with you."

Zach rolled her to her back and kissed her deeply. The embers of desire flared back to life as soon as his lips touched hers. He cupped her breast in his hand and rubbed his thumb over the nipple.

"You do realize that since we'll be living together, we'll make love a lot more often."

His little temptress smiled wickedly and wrapped her arms around his neck. "I certainly hope so."

The End

About the Author

ℌ

Lynn LaFleur's writing career has included winning several writing contests. She was a semi-finalist twice in the prestigious Golden Heart Contest of Romance Writers of America. She served on the board of the RWA Chapter in Sacramento, California, for four years, as secretary and activities director.

Lynn can't imagine ever writing anything except romances. "I love writing about a man and a woman falling in love. If you enjoy the story I tell enough to smile in places, shed a tear at times, or get a warm and fuzzy feeling, that is my greatest reward."

After living on the West Coast for twenty-one years, Lynn is back in Texas. She works for her small-town newspaper during the day and writes books of romance at night.

Lynn welcomes mail from readers. You can write to her c/o Ellora's Cave Publishing at 1056 Home Avenue, Akron OH 44310-3502.

Also by Lynn LaFleur

Ellora's Cavemen: Legendary Tails I *(anthology)*

Enchanted Rogues (*anthology*)

Happy Birthday, Baby

Holiday Heat (*anthology)*

One Night of Pleasure

Two Men and a Lady (*anthology)*

Why an electronic book?

We live in the Information Age—an exciting time in the history of human civilization in which technology rules supreme and continues to progress in leaps and bounds every minute of every hour of every day. For a multitude of reasons, more and more avid literary fans are opting to purchase e-books instead of paperbacks. The question to those not yet initiated to the world of electronic reading is simply: *why?*

1. *Price.* An electronic title at Ellora's Cave Publishing and Cerridwen Press runs anywhere from 40-75% less than the cover price of the exact same title in paperback format. Why? Cold mathematics. It is less expensive to publish an e-book than it is to publish a paperback, so the savings are passed along to the consumer.
2. *Space.* Running out of room to house your paperback books? That is one worry you will never have with electronic novels. For a low one-time cost, you can purchase a handheld computer designed specifically for e-reading purposes. Many e-readers are larger than the average handheld, giving you plenty of screen room. Better yet, hundreds of titles can be stored within your new library—a single microchip. (Please note that Ellora's Cave and Cerridwen Press does not endorse any specific brands. You can check our website at www.ellorascave.com or

www.cerridwenpress.com for customer recommendations we make available to new consumers.)

3. *Mobility.* Because your new library now consists of only a microchip, your entire cache of books can be taken with you wherever you go.
4. *Personal preferences are accounted for.* Are the words you are currently reading too small? Too large? Too...**ANNOYING**? Paperback books cannot be modified according to personal preferences, but e-books can.
5. *Instant gratification.* Is it the middle of the night and all the bookstores are closed? Are you tired of waiting days—sometimes weeks—for online and offline bookstores to ship the novels you bought? Ellora's Cave Publishing sells instantaneous downloads 24 hours a day, 7 days a week, 365 days a year. Our e-book delivery system is 100% automated, meaning your order is filled as soon as you pay for it.

Those are a few of the top reasons why electronic novels are displacing paperbacks for many an avid reader. As always, Ellora's Cave and Cerridwen Press welcomes your questions and comments. We invite you to email us at service@ellorascave.com, service@cerridwenpress.com or write to us directly at: 1056 Home Ave. Akron OH 44310-3502.

Cerridwen, the Celtic Goddess of wisdom, was the muse who brought inspiration to storytellers and those in the creative arts. Cerridwen Press encompasses the best and most innovative stories in all genres of today's fiction. Visit our site and discover the newest titles by talented authors who still get inspired - much like the ancient storytellers did, once upon a time.

Discover for yourself why readers can't get enough of the multiple award-winning publisher Ellora's Cave.

Whether you prefer e-books or paperbacks, be sure to visit EC on the web at www.ellorascave.com for an erotic reading experience that will leave you breathless.